GW00854583

Leo the Elf Saves Christmas

Bradley Doxon

First paperback edition October 2023

Paperback: 979-8-9888658-1-0

Hardcover: 979-8-8683195-3-2

Ebook: 979-8-9888658-0-3

www.bradleydoxon.com

For my wonderful children and my beautiful wife.
Thank you for all your inspiration.

Prologue

Banishment of the Sorrow King

S anta Claus sat on his golden throne, his long white beard flowing down his chest like a snowy waterfall. In front of him stood the Elder Elves, wise guardians of the Christmas Spirit. Worried looks spread across their faces as they waited for Santa to begin.

"I have called you here to discuss a threat that casts a shadow over our land," said Santa Claus. "A darkness is spreading that I fear is the work of the Sorrow King."

The Sorrow King was once the charming wizard king of the aptly named Wizard Realm before he fell victim to the clutches of dark magic. All light drained from the Wizard Realm, transforming it into a world of darkness. The Sorrow King became a frightening figure with a skeletal

1

face and fiery red eyes. He spent his days plotting ways to replace happiness with unending misery, as his powers came from the pain and suffering of others. Under his ruthlessness and hatred, the previously vibrant Wizard Realm withered into the Dark Realm.

Elder Oakbranch, the oldest of the twelve Elder Elves, stepped forward to address Santa. He wore a gray robe made of the finest unicorn hair, covered in beautiful symbols woven with gold threads.

"Santa, we must act quickly to protect the Christmas Spirit," said Elder Oakbranch. "The return of the Sorrow King will bring great suffering to the world if we do not stop him."

Santa Claus nodded. "You are correct, my dear Oakbranch. We must find the Sorrow King immediately and use our powers to drive him from our land. But we must be careful, for his dark magic is unpredictable."

"Do we know where he is?" asked Elder Willowbloom. She was the next oldest of the Elder Elves and second in command. Her long white hair fell over her shoulders and down her gray robe in two braids.

"My scouts last saw him near the frozen lakes south of the North Pole," said Santa Claus. "But he is not alone. The Sorrow King has brought with him his Despair Minions. Disgusting creatures that follow his every command."

"Are you sure this is wise, Santa Claus?" asked Elder Oakbranch.

Santa closed his eyes and connected with the ancient energy known as the Christmas Spirit. The Christmas Spirit lives in almost everything. People and animals have it, and so do trees and grass. Even the air we breathe carries the Christmas Spirit. It's the reason children can't sleep on Christmas Eve and why adults love to give gifts to one another. Even now, Santa felt his connection weaken as the Sorrow King destroyed the festive energy.

"The clock is ticking," Santa warned urgently. "The Sorrow King has already started his rampage. We must hurry."

Santa and the Elder Elves boarded his sleigh and set out to find the Sorrow King. Rudolph and his fellow reindeer pulled the sleigh, following a trail of misery leading to the frozen lakes. The fallen wizard was high atop a snowy hill, guarded by his black hyena-looking beasts. The reindeer brought the sleigh down to where the Sorrow King and his Despair Minions stood capturing the Christmas Spirit that filled the air.

"Halt, Sorrow King!" yelled Santa. "Your terror of darkness ends here."

The Sorrow King turned and faced Santa. "You cannot

3

stop me, Santa Claus!" His eyes filled with hatred. "The Christmas Spirit will wither and die at my touch."

The Elder Elves formed a circle around Santa, their hands glowing with magic.

"We stand for the power of love and joy," said Santa. "We will protect the Christmas Spirit with all our might!"

He raised his hands and called upon the very spirit of Christmas magic. Santa cast a powerful spell that sent waves of light flying toward the Sorrow King and his minions. The Sorrow King recoiled, his powers fading against the attack.

"You will not prevail!" shouted Santa. "Return to the realm of darkness whence you came!"

As the words left Santa's lips, a brilliant burst of light swallowed the Sorrow King. He cried out as Santa and the Elder Elves used their powers to banish him to the Dark Realm.

"We saved Christmas!" Santa Claus exclaimed, his laughter ringing through the air. "The light of the Christmas Spirit shines brighter than ever!"

With the Sorrow King secured in the Dark Realm, Santa and the Elder Elves returned to Santa's castle.

They gathered in a room beneath the castle, with large tapestries covering the walls in colorful greens and reds. In the center of the room was a circular table, its wooden top shining from the glow of the chandelier hanging above. Thirteen chairs surrounded the table; each carved with decorative candy canes and mistletoe.

Santa and the Elder Elves joined hands at the table and channeled their magic to form a barrier surrounding the Dark Realm.

"The Sorrow King can never escape the Dark Realm," said Santa. "The Christmas Spirit must remain strong and true. That is the only way we can be sure the Sorrow King will spend his life in captivity."

From that moment on, Santa Claus promised to bring the children of the Human Realm every gift they asked for. Even the ones on Santa's naughty list had presents to open on Christmas morning! He believed that would be the best way to prevent the Christmas Spirit from fading.

But Santa and the Elder Elves did not realize how powerful the Sorrow King was. Even though his body was trapped in the Dark Realm, his dark magic passed through the barrier. It slowly traveled the world and turned the people of the Human Realm against Santa Claus. Year after year, children grew tired of receiving every gift they asked for. Adults lost interest in the holiday as they relied on Santa Claus to provide presents.

With the treasured Christmas Spirit still threatened, Santa and the Elder Elves devised a plan. They would search for a great warrior capable of protecting the realms from the evil Sorrow King. They found their guardian in one of Santa's helper elves.

THE GUARDIAN ELF

I n the enchanted land of the North Pole stood Santa Claus's castle. Snowflakes danced and icicles sparkled in this place of wonder and magic. Hundreds of happy elves lived in the castle where they spent their days making toys and wrapping presents.

The elves were always jolly, singing and laughing as they worked. They were the best toy makers in all the realms, and millions of children loved their creations. Santa and Mrs. Claus spent their time watching over the elves throughout the year. Santa guided the elves in their work while Mrs. Claus baked delicious gingerbread cookies.

Among the hundreds of elves was the spirited Leo, Santa's most trusted elf. Like all elves, Leo's eyes were a bright shade of blue that sparkled in the sun, and his smile gave proof of his charming personality. But he was no ordinary elf. Leo stood about a head taller than the other elves. He was also much stronger and quicker than the rest. All the elves looked up to Leo, wishing they could someday be like him.

But what truly made Leo special were Everblade and Lumina, his sword and magical scepter. Everblade was a legendary sword designed and built by Santa himself. Forged with the finest steel in the North Pole, the sword could cut through almost anything. Lumina was an ancient scepter passed down to Leo by the Elder Elves. Its staff came from a branch off the oldest tree in the North Pole. One end of the staff held a crystal shard that could create light and ice.

One snowy morning, Leo jumped out of bed full of excitement. He slipped into his green elf suit and crammed on his green and red hat. Leo's big pointy ears stuck out from the sides of his hat. He raced through the castle halls searching for Santa Claus, grinning from pointy ear to pointy ear. Leo found Santa in his workshop, surrounded by toys awaiting their journey.

Leo and Santa Claus spent their days in the cozy workshop preparing for the most wonderful night of the year: Christmas Eve. Santa made toys, and Leo stood alert and ready to help. They also enjoyed the occasional gingerbread cookie or two.

Their friendship was strong, built through the years over fits of laughter, secrets, and of course, countless cups of hot cocoa. Santa trusted Leo with his life. Leo dedicated himself to protecting Santa and the Christmas Spirit with complete loyalty. Santa's mission was to bring joy and wonder to children everywhere, and Leo was to protect that mission from any threat.

Families around the world waited with anticipation for the gifts Santa would bring. Boys and girls knew from an early age that they had to be good and kind to each other to make sure they were on Santa's good list.

"Good morning, Santa!" Leo exclaimed in an excited voice as he entered the workshop.

Santa looked up from the toy he was building. "Ah, there's my trusty guardian elf!"

"Santa, I have a brilliant idea that will make this Christmas the most amazing ever!" Leo grinned.

Santa chuckled, his belly jiggling like a bowl full of jelly. "Oh, do tell me, Leo. I'm all ears."

Leo leaned over and whispered, "Santa, I've been thinking. What if we created a brand new kind of toy that anyone could wear? I've got a great name for them: Giggle Goggles. They'll have funny antennae and a button you can push that will send the wearer into hysterical fits of giggles!"

"Oh, Leo, you never fail to bring joy and wonder with your incredible ideas!" Santa chuckled. "I can already imagine the sound of laughter filling the air."

Mrs. Claus appeared with a tray of cookies fresh from the oven. Their sweet aroma wafted through the air as Mrs. Claus entered the room.

"My dears," said Mrs. Claus. "I thought you might need some sweet treats to fuel your creativity!"

Leo's pointed ears perked up, and his eyes widened in delight. "Are those gingerbread cookies? Thank you, Mrs. Claus!"

With his mouth full of cookie, Leo clumsily said goodbye to Santa and Mrs. Claus and left the workshop.

When he was not with Santa in the shop, Leo practiced his skills with his shiny sword and magic scepter each morning. He went straight to the training yard outside Santa's castle where the elves could unleash their inner magic. A sturdy wooden fence surrounded the training area. The fence bore gashes and cuts from countless past training sessions. Inside the fence was a wide-open space shaped like a circle. A thick layer of fresh snow covered the ground, creating a soft surface that absorbed the impact of every leap and fall.

Leo made his way to the center of the training yard. Curious elves gathered around the fence to watch the spectacle that was about to unfold.

Leo concentrated as he swung his sword, pretending to protect Santa's castle from evil creatures. His muscles flexed as he dashed around the training yard, dodging and striking the imaginary enemies.

He turned to his left and reached for Lumina, his magical scepter. Leo gripped Lumina, feeling a tingle of energy flow through his fingers. With a wave of his scepter, Leo summoned a gust of wind. Snow and leaves swirled in the air, creating a mini-tornado. The other elves giggled with excitement as the wind tickled their cheeks.

Then, with a playful flick of his hand, Leo summoned tiny pellets of ice around Lumina's crystal shard. They danced along the wooden staff like tiny snowflakes. He carefully shot streams of pellets into the sky, avoiding the now enormous crowd of elves.

Leo could feel his skills improving the more he practiced. He swung his sword with more accuracy, and his scepter obeyed his every command. Leo knew that with plenty of practice and a little bit of patience, he would be ready to face any challenge.

A voice boomed near the castle's entrance, "Back to work!" A hush fell over the yard. Leo paused mid-swing as he and the other elves turned to find the source of the loud voice. Just beyond the yard was Santa Claus, standing as stiff as a statue with his arms crossed.

The crowd of elves followed Santa into the castle with their heads hung low. Leo remained in the training yard, unsure what had come over his old friend to make him act like that.

Mrs. Claus baked more cookies and tidied up around the castle. Still, she couldn't shake her worries. Something seemed wrong with Santa, and she had to find Leo.

Mrs. Claus spotted Leo amid the chaos in Santa's workshop. His green hat was tilted slightly to the side. He was deep in concentration, putting together thousands of Giggle Goggles, trying on each pair before moving on to the next. Mrs. Claus rushed over and patted him on the shoulder, looking concerned.

"Hey, Leo," she said in a worried tone. "Do you think there's something wrong with Santa? Have you noticed him acting strange?"

Leo frowned and thought hard. He scratched his pointy ears as he recalled the events of the day.

"Well, Mrs. Claus," said Leo. "I was in the training

yard this morning, practicing with Everblade and Lumina. The other elves were watching as usual, but Santa got all grumpy and told them to get back to work. He's usually all about having fun, you know?"

Mrs. Claus nodded. Try as she might, she couldn't hide her concern.

"Oh, my dear Leo," she sighed. "That is not like Santa at all. He loves to see you elves playing and having fun. Can you go talk to Santa and see what's bothering him? Your friendship means the world to him. Perhaps you can help."

"Absolutely, Mrs. Claus!" Leo exclaimed. "I'll head straight to Santa's study right now and find out what's bugging him."

Mrs. Claus beamed at Leo as he scampered toward the study. Leo's heart pounded as he tapped on the door, waiting for Santa's invitation to enter.

"Come in," Santa said from inside the room.

Leo pushed the door open and stepped into Santa's study. Santa sat in his favorite armchair positioned in front of the crackling fire. A soft light bounced up and down the room, as if the shadows seemed to be playing a game of hide-and-seek.

Santa watched the dancing flames as Leo approached. "I apologize for my outburst earlier, Leo, but Christmas Eve is only three days away. We must hurry if we are to have these toys ready for the good boys and girls of the world!"

"Relax, Santa," said Leo. "We've never missed a Christmas before. This year won't be any different."

Santa sighed and replied, "You're right, my dear friend. But you know how nervous I get this time of year."

Leo smiled as he handed Santa a pair of his Giggle Goggles. "Between you, me, and the rest of the elves, Christmas will be a success. I promise."

It was clear from the look on Santa's face that he was still worried.

"Leo, my faithful guardian," he put his hand on Leo's shoulder. "I fear I have not been as honest with you as I should have been."

"What do you mean, Santa?" asked Leo.

"Hundreds of years ago, dark magic turned the king of the Wizard Realm evil," said Santa. "He became known as the Sorrow King. Hatred fueled his soul, and his goal was to destroy the Christmas Spirit. But the Elder Elves and I stopped him before he was successful. We used our magic to form a powerful barrier that trapped the Sorrow King and his minions inside the Dark Realm."

"Why don't you have the Elder Elves to help you again?" asked Leo.

"Our barrier has weakened over the years, and the Sorrow King's power has grown stronger," said Santa.

"And I can not leave the elves alone in the castle this close to Christmas."

"But why me, Santa?"

"The Elder Elves and I agreed more defensive measures were needed," said Santa. "That is where you come in. Yes, you are my protector. But we have also chosen you as the last line of defense for the Christmas Spirit."

"What do you want me to do?" asked Leo.

"As my trusted guardian, I am asking you to go on a journey to speak with the Elder Elves and ask for their guidance. Travel to the Mystic Forest past the walls of my castle. There you will find the Elder Elves. We put a stop to the Sorrow King before, and now I fear we must do so again. We must protect the Christmas Spirit at all costs."

"Do not worry, Santa," he replied. "I will be your shield. I will face this darkness and see that the Christmas Spirit endures."

AVA

- -

Ava Slacks stared out her bedroom window at the snow-covered town below. Her breath created foggy circles on the glass as she looked out the window. The sight of the softly falling snow filled her with bubbling excitement.

"Christmas is almost here!" Ava whispered in delight. "Too bad no one else in this stupid town cares." With a sigh, she pulled the curtains of her window shut.

Ava went downstairs and found her father standing in the living room, surrounded by toys.

"Daddy, are all these toys for me?" she asked. Her father, Michael Slacks, smiled weakly as he addressed Ava. "Afraid not, sweetie. These are the extra toys for our store in case we sell out of all the others."

"Oh, but why are they here?"

"Well, I haven't sold a single toy all season," he frowned. "Nobody seems to be in the Christmas spirit this year."

"But I still feel it, Daddy. I feel the magic of Christmas in my heart."

Michael knelt and looked into Ava's eyes. "You are a special girl, Ava. Your spirit shines bright, even when the lights of others have dimmed."

Ava sighed, not satisfied with his explanation. She wanted everyone in town to feel the same excitement she felt. Ava was determined to take matters into her own hands. She came up with a plan she knew would put everyone in the Christmas spirit. Ava gathered her markers and a large sheet of cardboard and started to draw. She drew Christmas trees and snowflakes, chocolate chip cookies and gingerbread houses, candy canes and presents. Then she wrote big letters across the board and colored them in bright greens and reds. *If this doesn't get people in the Christmas spirit again, I don't know what will,* thought Ava.

With the last bow drawn to perfection on a red and gold gift, Ava had finished her work. She picked up her sign, slipped on her red snow boots and green winter coat, and bounded out the door. She raced through the busy streets of her town, smiling the entire time.

Ava stood in front of the town square holding her sign that read, "Bring back the Christmas Spirit!" People passing by glanced at her curiously but continued on their way, ignoring her sign's plea.

Then Ava approached a couple walking by. "Excuse me, have you felt the Christmas Spirit lately?" she asked.

They looked puzzled when they heard Ava's question. "Is it really Christmas already?" the woman asked.

"Christmas is only three days away! Didn't you know that?" Ava asked, looking up at the man who had a confused look on his face.

"I...uh, guess we forgot," the man said. "Maybe we'll celebrate next year."

"Thanks..." Ava's heart sank, but she refused to give up. She ran up to a group of children playing in the park and asked, "Hey, do you remember the joy of Christmas? The excitement of presents and caroling?"

The children shrugged, uninterested in what Ava had to say.

"Not really," said one child.

"Santa already brought us everything we asked for last year," said another.

"Yeah, and I don't like singing Christmas carols," said another. "They're boring."

"But Christmas is so much more than opening

presents," Ava grumbled. "It's about love and joy and being with your loved ones!"

A white ball flew toward Ava, but she was too distracted to see it in time. The snowball made a thud as it collided with her sign.

"We see our families all year long," said the child who threw the snowball. "There's nothing special 'bout Christmas that makes them any better

Ava felt she was not making any progress. She spotted an elderly woman daydreaming on a nearby bench. Ava's face filled with hope as she approached the woman.

"Do you remember how magical Christmas used to be?"

The woman smiled at Ava. "Yes, dear. I remember those days. But it seems like they're long gone."

Ava slumped her shoulders as the weight of disappointment washed over her. *Why doesn't anyone in this stupid town believe in the magic of Christmas?* thought Ava. As she walked back home, her steps were heavy, her mind filled with questions.

She slammed the front door as she stomped into her house. Ava could feel the warmth of her home, but her heart felt cold. The toys from earlier that morning still littered the living room floor. Her father sat in his cozy leather chair, reading the local newspaper as she entered the room.

Michael looked up from the newspaper he was holding and saw the sadness in Ava's eyes.

"Hey, sweetheart. How did it go?" he asked gently, worried about his daughter.

Ava let out a deep sigh. "Terribly, Dad. Nobody seemed to care about bringing back the Christmas Spirit. It's like they've all forgotten what Christmas even is," she said.

Michael reached out and placed a comforting hand on Ava's shoulder. "I know it's hard, Ava. But sometimes...people need a little nudge to remind them of the joy and magic of Christmas. You tried your best. That's what matters most."

Ava nodded. She always appreciated her father's attempts to lift her spirits, even if she could still see the sadness in his eyes. It was hard for them both to watch the Christmas Spirit fade in their town.

"I just thought I could make a difference, Dad," Ava whispered. "And bring back the joy and happiness."

Michael hugged her tightly. "You are making a difference, Ava. Your belief will inspire others, even if they don't show it right away. Don't give up hope."

"I wish mom were still here; she'd know what to do," Ava said. A single tear rolled down her cheek. "Christmas was her favorite time of year. Remember all the decorations she'd put out?"

Michael smiled at the thought. "You could hardly move in this house without knocking over a snowman. And she always had a Santa Claus hiding in every room."

"And the lights! I bet you could see our house from space," Ava said and managed a small laugh.

"What do you think?" Michael asked. "Do you want to dust off that box of decorations and make this house festive again?"

"Not right now, Dad. I think I just need some time alone in my room."

"Of course, sweetheart," he said. "Take all the time you need. You know where I'll be if you need me." As she turned to go upstairs, Michael gave her a gentle pat on the back.

Ava went into her room and closed the door behind her, then fell flat on her bed. She stared out the window as clouds drifted by, ignoring the very upsetting day she just had.

That night, as Ava lay in bed, she closed her eyes and whispered into the quiet room, "I'm not going to give up, Christmas Spirit. The whole world needs to feel your magic again. I'll find a way to bring you back if it's the last thing I do."

And so, as the snowflakes danced outside her window, Ava was determined to reignite the Christmas Spirit in the hearts of the people in her town.

Deep within the Dark Realm, the Sorrow King sat upon his sinister throne inside his fortress. His eyes glowed red with excitement as he felt the outside realms shifting.

"The Christmas Spirit is fading," his voice echoed through the dark chamber. "As the light of joy and happiness fades, my powers grow stronger."

With a flick of his hand, the Sorrow King summoned his loyal Despair Minions. The room filled with glowing red eyes as the creatures appeared.

"My faithful minions," he said. "It is time for us to make another journey into the Human Realm. Their joy is fading, and we will feast upon their despair!"

The Despair Minions nodded eagerly.

"We have a score to settle with a certain jolly elf and his red suit."

The Sorrow King rose from his throne and raised his skeletal hand. A shadowy portal formed and swirled in the darkness. The Despair Minions followed their evil leader as he stepped through the portal and entered the Human Realm.

CAVE OF WONDER

Leo thought his mission was simple enough: locate the Elder Elves and find a way to save Christmas. He tightened his belt and made sure Lumina and Everblade were secure. Satisfied, Leo took off down the snowy hill from Santa's castle that led straight into the Mystic Forest.

He had never traveled this far from the castle before. In fact, no elf had ever left the castle grounds. Everything they needed was given to them by Santa and Mrs. Claus. The new landscape and strange surroundings filled Leo with excitement.

The trees of the Mystic Forest were even bigger than Leo had imagined. He thought it was funny the way distance made things look smaller than they were. A wall of trees stretched as far as Leo could see. He looked to his left and right, searching for a way through. A narrow trail snaked its way through the trees just to his right. The forest was dark, aside from the faint glow coming from strange flowers that lined the sides of the path.

"This is it," Leo said. "The Mystic Forest. Here goes nothing."

He followed the glowing flowers deeper and deeper. Through the cover of the trees, Leo caught glimpses of deer and other creatures he couldn't quite make out. All around him, the forest teemed with life and the sounds of passing animals. He couldn't shake the feeling that he was being watched by someone–or something.

The path led him to a clearing that stretched about fifty feet in both directions. Sunlight penetrated the space, providing Leo with a sense of calmness. A hush fell over the surrounding trees when Leo entered the clearing.

The largest tree he had ever seen cast a shadow straight down the middle of the clearing. Leo stared in amazement at its branches that reached high into the sunny sky. Then he noticed movement down at the base of the tree. Twelve elves stood under the tall tree, wearing gray robes that flowed the ground.

"We have been expecting you, young guardian," said Elder Oakbranch. "You have come seeking our knowledge, no?"

"What do you know of the Sorrow King and the Dark Realm?" asked Leo as he bowed to the Elder Elves. "Santa believes his powers are growing stronger by the day and that he threatens the very existence of Christmas."

The wise elves formed a circle around Leo and spoke in unison. "With light, there must be darkness. The Christmas Spirit is our light; the Sorrow King is our darkness," their voices trailed off. An enchanted light flowed from Leo as visions of evil spirits danced around him. "The Christmas Spirit is more than a feeling. It is a living being, a force capable of power beyond your imagination. It lives inside everything you see and can be found in places you least expect. The Sorrow King and his Despair Minions are powerless as long as the Christmas Spirit remains strong and true."

Leo watched the light flowing from his body push back the evil spirits surrounding him. One by one, the spirits vanished as the Elder Elves spoke.

"Tragically, our worlds have grown resentful of Christmas. Envy and bitterness have replaced joy and laughter. Children no longer look forward to Santa's arrival. Mothers and fathers no longer teach their children kindness and charity. And so, the Sorrow King grows stronger." Leo's light grew fainter and fainter, allowing the evil spirits to close in on him. Then the light disappeared, and Leo found himself engulfed in darkness. His heart was pounding, and sweat gathered on his brow. Evil whispers that filled Leo with fear and dread echoed from every direction.

"How can he be stopped?" asked Leo. "How do we save the world from the Sorrow King and restore the Christmas Spirit?"

"The Sorrow King and the Despair Minions are mighty adversaries," said Elder Willowbloom. "However, the Christmas Spirit is a powerful force that cannot be easily extinguished. If one person still believes in its magic, the Christmas Spirit will live on. The world is relying on you to keep it alive, Leo. Deep within this forest is a hidden place we call the Cave of Wonder. That cave holds one of many keys you will need on your quest." The Elder Elves turned and vanished into the dense forest.

Noises from animals slowly came back to life. Leo found a second trail of glowing flowers opposite where he had entered the clearing. He walked along the snow-covered ground until he came to a fork.

He stared at the split in the path, unsure of which way to go. The flowers lined both directions, each beckoning him forward. Leo closed his eyes and concentrated. *The Elder Elves never said it would be this hard,* thought Leo. *Give me a hint. Just one hint. Please.* Leo begged, then shivered as a sudden breeze pushed him from behind. He opened his eyes and knew which way to go. Leo turned and began walking down the path to his left.

Decorations were hanging from every corner of the living room by the time Ava woke up. Michael worked tirelessly the whole night to surprise his daughter. He was stringing up the last set of lights as she walked downstairs.

Ava's mouth dropped at the festive sight. Everywhere she looked were snowmen and angels, reindeer and mistletoe, Santa Claus and his elves.

"Good morning, sweetheart!" Michael said. "What do you think?"

"It's amazing, Daddy," said Ava. "Mom would be so happy!" She ran to her father and hugged him tight, careful not to disturb his decorations.

"I thought this would make you happy."

"You have no idea," she said, her eyes filling with tears as she looked around the room.

"I'm so glad you like it, sweetheart," Michael said. "Now I have to go to work, so go out there and try to have some fun."

"I will, Daddy," she said. "I promise."

Her father's hard work had inspired Ava to go back to the town square and once again try to put others in the Christmas Spirit.

She stood proudly among the crowd of kids scattered about, holding her sign and singing carols. A group of three boys noticed Ava and came up to her with big grins on their faces.

"Hey, Ava," sneered Timothy Daniels, the oldest one in the group. "Back out here with your stupid sign again, huh?"

Ava did her best to hide the sign behind her jacket. "What do you care, *Timothy*?" Ava asked. "It's not for you, anyway."

"Come on," he said as he grabbed for the sign. "Let me see it!"

The other two boys grabbed Ava's arms as Timothy ripped the sign from her hands.

He read the sign. "'Bring back the Christmas Spirit!' Do you really think a few dumb words are going to make any difference?" Timothy ripped Ava's hard work in half and dropped it on the ground. The other boys joined him as they walked away laughing.

Ava fell to the ground and picked up the pieces of her sign. Tears streamed down her face as she tried to put it back together.

"You're going to get what's coming to you, Timothy Daniels!" she yelled in exasperation. The other children in the town square passed her by, playing their boring games, while Ava sat crying on the cold ground.

Heavy snow fell on the floor of the forest. Leo shielded his eyes from the pounding ice, an unwelcome guest on this difficult journey. He did his best to scan the area in search of the cave's entrance, but the snow was coming down too hard to make out anything. The trees up ahead stretched on for what seemed like forever, disappearing inside a wide open mouth.

"That has to be the Cave of Wonder," said Leo. He sprinted through the raging blizzard, desperately wanting to get out of the blinding snow. The path of trees and glowing flowers ended outside the cave's entrance. He placed his hands on Everblade and Lumina, then stepped into the cave. All sound disappeared aside from the constant drip of water echoing from the depths. Dampness and mildew filled Leo's nose when he breathed the cave's stale air. He held his breath and took a step deeper into the cave.

He had traveled only a few feet before the darkness

swallowed him whole. Leo turned to find the entrance to the cave, but all he could see was black emptiness. He gripped Lumina tight as he muttered a quick spell. A faint light shone from Lumina's crystal, but the darkness proved too powerful for the spell. *Guess I'm doing this the hard way,* thought Leo.

Leo stumbled and pushed his way through the Cave of Wonder. The darkness was so thick that he could not see the light from Lumina.

"Where is that key?" Leo said to himself.

Suddenly, the ground beneath his feet gave way, and Leo fell down a deep shaft. His screams bounced off the rocky walls as he tumbled through the darkness. Leo reached for something, anything he could grasp, but he was falling too fast. Then Leo landed at the bottom of the shaft with a thud. He was relieved that he wasn't hurt, but his body still ached. A faint glow coming from the side wall caught Leo's attention as he caught his breath. Curiosity getting the better of him, Leo dragged himself toward the light.

Nestled among the shadows was a small stone that seemed to pulse some mystical energy, filling the cave with a soft green light. With wonder in his eyes, Leo reached down and picked up the glowing stone.

A surge of energy shot from his hand to all parts of his body the instant he touched the stone. Leo could sense it was connected to something greater. Something ancient. Something powerful. *This must be the key the Elder Elves told me to find,* thought Leo. He carefully tucked the stone in the pocket of his tunic and pushed it in deep to make sure it was secure.

The cave went farther down than Leo had expected. A rocky wall stopped Leo in his tracks. *End of the road, I guess,* thought Leo. He reached up and felt a ledge that was just wide enough to pull himself onto. Leo stepped onto the narrow ledge, making sure he wouldn't be in for another surprise fall. His pounding heart made it hard to steady himself along the ledge. He managed to get his fingers inside the rough edges enough to climb.

The jagged rocks scraped against Leo's hands as he went higher. The slippery surface made each step riskier than the last. Leo reached the top of the wall and pulled himself up from the claustrophobic passage. He searched for a way out, looking around every corner and behind piles of fallen rocks.

Leo turned toward a distant alcove where a faint white glow caught his eye. At first, he thought his eyes were playing tricks on him. He blinked three times, but the light was still there. Leo sprinted forward to find the source.

Fifty yards later, a path came into view that led to the cave's exit. Leo ran out of the cave into a grassy clearing and took a deep breath of fresh air. The echoes of the cave were far behind him now. Ahead of Leo was a bustling city with busy streets and crowded sidewalks.

THE STRIPPED CHRISTMAS SPIRIT

L eo was now in the Human Realm. The realm where Santa Claus traveled every Christmas Eve to deliver presents to all the good boys and girls–even the naughty ones! The realm where the Christmas Spirit lived and thrived. Yet something felt wrong. A deep emptiness hung in the air as if the Christmas Spirit had been stripped away.

Across the street was Slack's Toy Store. The lights were on but a "CLOSED" sign hung on the door. A man sat alone behind the counter, his head hanging low. Leo tucked his pointy ears under his hat to hide his identity as best he could and crossed the busy street.

Michael Slacks sat behind the counter as he

contemplated whether to unlock the door or not. He was the tenth owner of the 200-year-old toy store. Michael's father owned the store before him, and his father before him, and his father before him, and so on. Michael checked his watch for the eighth time in less than two minutes.

Leo went to the door and peeked inside. Toys filled the shelves and cases throughout the store.

"Christmas is only a few days away," Leo wondered out loud. "Why aren't the shelves empty?" He watched as Michael looked at his watch again, and then Leo tapped the glass. Michael's eyes lit up as he turned to the door where Leo was standing. Michael thought Leo was a little kid in a Christmas outfit. He jumped out of his seat and ran to let Leo inside.

"Well, hello! Come on in! What can I help you find today? Are you looking for a dinosaur? Or perhaps a pair of roller skates?"

"I'm sorry, sir, but I'm not here to shop," said Leo. "I am curious, though. Why are your shelves still full of toys? Christmas is almost here. Aren't people still excited?"

Michael gave Leo a puzzled look.

"Where are you from, kid? The North Pole? No one here has been excited about Christmas for years! What's the point of giving each other presents if Santa Claus gives everyone what they want?"

Leo's heart sank. He could not believe what he was hearing. Had humans forgotten the meaning of Christmas?

"But sir, Christmas is the special time of year when humans share the joy of giving gifts and spending time with the ones they love!" Leo proclaimed. "Keeping the Christmas Spirit alive by spreading cheer and goodwill to one another!"

"Look around you, kid. Does it look like anyone is in the Christmas spirit anymore? Do you hear any carolers singing songs? Do you see any lights or trees decorated in store windows? No ugly sweaters, no Santa hats, no mistletoe. Heck, I don't think I've seen a kid build a snowman in years! Even my daughter, as hard as she's tried to stay in the Christmas spirit, is close to giving up all hope this year. The Christmas Spirit is gone, my friend. And I don't think it's coming back."

Leo thought about what he had heard and asked, "Your daughter? Where is she now?"

"Ava?" Michael replied. "She's probably down at the town square holding up that sign of hers. Poor girl, she's spent the last two days trying to get others in the Christmas spirit. But no one seems to be interested this year."

"Don't worry," said Leo. "I think there may be a way to save the Christmas Spirit. Thanks!" Leo spun around and headed out the door still marked "CLOSED."

"Wait, don't you want to buy a toy?" called Michael, but Leo was already gone. Michael looked down at his watch one last time, then flipped the sign over to "OPEN," and sat back down behind the counter. This time with a little hope in his heart.

Leo tore through the crowd that lined the street. He passed stores with no holiday decorations, their shelves filled with mundane items. Christmas lights drooped unlit from lampposts. Children's eyes lacked the spark of wonder, and the warmth of giving had grown cold.

Leo reached the town square and stared in disbelief at the scene. At least a hundred children of all ages crowded the area. Some children made snow angels while others threw snowballs at each other. But none of the children seemed to be having any fun. Snowballs exploded on jackets with a small "thwush" but nothing else. No laughter. No squeals of joy. No "Hey, watch it!" Just silence.

How am I supposed to find Ava? thought Leo. *Guess I'll have to do this the hard way.* Leo approached the nearest child and asked, "Do you believe in the magic of Christmas?"

Instead of a resounding "Of course I do," Leo was met with "Beat it, kid." So Leo went to another.

"Do you believe in the magic of Christmas?"

"Scram!"

"Do you believe in the magic of Christmas?"

"Christmas is stupid!"

"Do you believe in the magic of Christmas?"

"Christmas is dumb!"

"Do you believe in the magic of Christmas?"

"Who cares about Christmas?"

One by one, the children dismissed Leo's question. The Christmas Spirit was all but gone. He scanned the town square for any sign of hope until his eyes fell on a little girl dressed in the reds and greens of Christmas. She was taller than Leo, which came as no surprise (even though Leo *was* the tallest elf), and looked to be about nine years old. Her strawberry blonde hair fell in curls, poking out from under her red hat. Leo could sense her genuine love for Christmas. He went to the girl and whispered, "Do you believe in the magic of Christmas?"

Ava's eyes widened in surprise as she turned to face Leo. "I do," she whispered, her voice filled with wonder and uncertainty. "But it feels like the magic is fading. I'm the only kid in this whole town who's excited about Christmas."

Leo smiled. "I know this sounds crazy, but what if I told you there was a way to bring back that magic?" he asked.

"Who are you?" Ava asked curiously. She looked at Leo's hat and his strange leather snow boots and thought something was wrong.

"I know *this* sounds crazy, but my name is Leo, and I come from the North Pole. I am Santa Claus's guardian elf."

Ava lit up with excitement. "You're one of Santa's helpers? What are you doing here?"

Leo nodded. "Indeed I am. I'm here on a mission to restore the Christmas Spirit and save Christmas. And I need your help."

"It's no use, Leo," said Ava. "I've tried to get others into the Christmas spirit, but no one seems to care."

"I know what you mean," said Leo. "But trust me, the two of us will have no problem convincing them."

Ava watched people pass by the town square, their heads held down low. Not one happy expression was found anywhere. Leo placed his hand on Ava's shoulder and smiled at her.

"It may seem like an uphill battle," said Leo. "But sometimes all it takes is a single spark to start a fire. We could be that spark, Ava."

Ava remembered the excitement she used to feel during Christmas and the joy the holiday spread to every corner of her town. *Can we truly rekindle that feeling? Can we bring back the magic that had been lost?* thought Ava.

"You're right," she said. "Okay. I'm willing to give it a shot."

"Thank you, Ava," said Leo. "You have no idea how much this will mean to Santa."

"So, where do we begin?"

"We'll start by reminding everyone of the wonders of Christmas and the happiness it brings," Leo said.

"And what if that doesn't work?" asked Ava.

"Let's just say I may have a little Christmas magic up my sleeve."

A stream sat deep in the forest on the outskirts of town. Sunlight danced across the water like a glittering ribbon, winding through the tall trees and frozen rocks. Pristine white snow blanketed the ground, giving the stream the appearance of a trail. A family of deer left small tracks in the snow as they approached the stream to drink. The doe lowered her head to the cool, rushing water and began to drink. Then her two fawns joined her and lowered their heads.

A cold breeze blew through the trees of the forest. The Sorrow King wore a black cloak that billowed in the icy wind. His pale face was filled with endless sadness, and his eyes glowed with a frightening light. The ground beneath him seemed to quiver in fear of his presence. The Sorrow King's minions slithered behind him. Their forms shifted and changed in an eerie dance as they moved.

The doe lifted her head from the cool water as the snow crunched around her. With a sudden jolt, the doe leaped from the stream and ran toward the trees. Her two fawns followed close behind.

The stream's once glistening surface became frozen and lifeless as the Sorrow King and his minions crept past. The vibrant blue water became trapped beneath a layer of ice. A dark fog followed the evil beings, blocking all light. The frigid air grew colder as if burdened by the weight of sorrow.

The Sorrow King loomed over the town where Leo and Ava met, casting a dark shadow across the horizon.

AVA'S PERIL

A va and Leo traveled the town hand-in-hand, their voices joining in joyful harmony as they sang Christmas carols. The festive tunes rang through the streets, touching the hearts of all who heard them.

"'Tis the season to be jolly, fa la la la la, la la la la!"

The atmosphere around them seemed to magically change. Once dull and gloomy streets were now adorned with twinkling lights, shimmering ornaments, and cheerful decorations. Laughter filled the air as children ran about carrying colorfully wrapped gifts.

Leo's question, "Do you believe in the magic of Christmas?" inspired everyone they greeted. Each person they met shared their memories of past Christmases and their excitement for the holiday ahead.

41

"Oh, how could I not believe in it?" said one man. "Christmas has a way of bringing out the best in people!"

"Christmas is the best time of the year!" said a sweet woman in a cozy red and green sweater. "It's when we come together to celebrate and make beautiful memories with the ones we love."

Smiles appeared on the faces of weary residents as they moved from house to house. Windows shimmered with the warm glow of holiday lights. Storefronts transformed into festive wonderlands with colorful decorations adorning walls and windows.

Twinkling lights and colorful displays caught the attention of passing crowds. Children stopped to stare in wonder at the giant inflatable Santa Claus now set up in the center of town. Adults walking by smiled as they remembered their own childhood Christmases. And the smell of freshly baked cookies filled the air. For a moment, the world seemed a little brighter.

At Slack's Toy Shop, a wave of excitement swept through the aisles. The laughter and chatter of eager customers filled the once-quiet place. Children's eyes sparkled with delight as they explored the shelves overflowing with toys and games. The magic of Christmas had returned, and the joyful spirit radiated from every corner of the store.

Ava and Leo were filled with joy and a sense of accomplishment as they watched the magic of Christmas come alive.

"It worked, Leo!" exclaimed Ava. "Everyone's happy again. We saved Christmas!"

Leo cracked a smile and put his arm around Ava's shoulder. "Here, in this town. But there are more places to save before Christmas Day. We should split up and continue spreading cheer to as many people as we can find."

"Split up?" Ava hesitated for a moment. "But Leo, look how much we have accomplished together in such a short time! Can't we keep going as a team?"

Leo smiled at his friend. "I appreciate your help, Ava. And the changes we've made together are incredible. But my journey is not complete, and there are more places in need of my magic."

"Why can't I come with you?"

"You have a unique gift, Ava," Leo said. "I know you can continue spreading cheer here. Bring joy to everyone you meet and keep the Christmas Spirit alive. I promise we will reunite once I have completed my mission."

Ava reluctantly went her separate way, in search of others to help spread the Christmas cheer. Leo ventured on, looking for the next town in need of his magic.

43

Under the cover of the nearby forest, the Sorrow King and his Despair Minions had watched Leo and Ava's every move. Ava's magic had caught their attention amidst the growing festive spirit. The Sorrow King's eyes narrowed and an evil grin formed on his face. With Ava alone and Leo gone, the Despair Minions began their sinister work. They slithered through the town, leaving a trail of despair in their wake. Flickering lights went dark. The air drained from the inflatable Santa Claus. Every step the Despair Minions took sucked the joy and cheer of Christmas from every corner of town.

The Sorrow King set his sights on Ava. He knew that capturing her would severely damage the newly restored Christmas Spirit. He moved toward Ava, ready to unleash his powers and plunge the town back into despair.

The air grew colder, and a threatening message blew through the air to Ava's ears. It was a warning. A terrifying voice spoke from dancing shadows.

"We are coming for you, little girl," the voice said.

Fear gripped Ava's heart, but she refused to be intimidated. She had seen the power of love and joy working with Leo and knew the Christmas Spirit was worth fighting for.

Ava turned down a dark street that was still untouched by the Christmas Spirit. Ignoring the voices, she continued to sing carols as she walked. "Deck the halls with boughs of holly! Fa-la-la-la-la La-la-la-la!"

Another voice rang out from behind Ava. She turned to see who it was, but no one was there. Just dark shadows dancing along the path she had crossed seconds before.

"Hello?" Ava asked. "Leo? Was that you?" The shadows continued their eerie dance.

Ava continued down the street, this time at a much faster pace and without caroling. The next street ahead of her was aglow with Christmas lights and fellow carolers.

I'll be safe if I can just make it there, thought Ava. Another gust of cold wind blew past, enveloping the world around her in darkness. A swirling vortex of shadows surrounded Ava, attempting to swallow her whole. The Despair Minions had found their target.

More menacing voices echoed from the darkness, "Hello, little girl. We've been watching you."

"What do you want from me?" Ava asked, pulling her jacket tighter to block the freezing air.

"Your Christmas Spirit," the voices echoed. "Give it to us."

Ava noticed a surge of light glowing from her body. Ava couldn't believe her eyes. *Where did that light come from?* she thought.

The Despair Minions circled Ava, inching closer and closer. Panic surged through her and the light glowing from her body began to flicker. Frozen hands grabbed her arms and legs, holding her in place.

"Let me go!" screamed Ava. She tried to fight back, but the Despair Minions gripped her tighter. Grief filled her heart as they drained the Christmas Spirit from her. Ava's blood ran frozen like a milkshake through a tiny straw. The glowing light had nearly faded away when a familiar voice rang out from behind her.

"Do you believe in the magic of Christmas?" Summoning his strength, Leo swung Everblade and sliced through the Despair Minions. The minions recoiled, their powers fading in the face of Leo's relentless attacks.

The Sorrow King remained hidden, watching their every move. His eyes burned with rage. He realized that his minions alone were not enough to stop the threat posed by Ava and Leo. An evil smile formed on the Sorrow King's face. He summoned a powerful spell, unleashing a force that threatened to trap them both.

Sensing the impending danger, Leo reached for Lumina.

"Ava! Get down!" Leo commanded as he channeled a wave of magic with his scepter to create a protective shield around them. The Sorrow King's spell slammed into the shield, creating a burst of light as bright as a hundred suns.

Leo used all the energy he could muster as he held Lumina, using its powers to protect them from the Sorrow King. But the spell unleashed by the evil being proved too much for Leo. His legs trembled under the unbearable weight pressed against him. Ava could see that something was wrong, and she came up behind the little elf and placed her hands on Lumina as well. With Ava's help, Leo launched a counterattack. A surge of magical energy shot out in all directions. The Despair Minions scattered, their miserable forms vanishing into nothingness.

Ava's gaze fell on Leo, who lay sprawled on the ground, his trusty weapons at his side.

"Leo, we're safe now. We won. Those...creatures, they're gone."

Leo groaned as he strained to pull himself to his feet. "What just happened? I thought we were done for!" He retrieved Everblade and Lumina and put them in their holsters on his belt.

"You were trying to protect us from whatever those

47

things were—"

"Despair Minions."

"But they were too strong, and you were struggling. That's when I grabbed your magic wand—"

"Lumina."

"Lumina...and a bright light erupted from it, and then those Despair Minions disappeared," said Ava. She scanned their surroundings for any sign of lingering danger. "Why were they after me, Leo?"

Leo lowered his head and traced patterns on the ground with his foot as he considered his response. *Is she ready to know why I'm on a mission to save Christmas? I guess it's too late now,* thought Leo.

"Santa Claus has assigned me a special mission: to save the Christmas Spirit. You see, the Christmas Spirit isn't just a feeling–it's a living being."

"That's why you came here, to bring the Christmas Spirit back to life?"

"Yes, exactly," Leo affirmed. "Its power protects our worlds from an evil being known as The Sorrow King. Unfortunately, the Christmas Spirit has faded in your realm. But no one knew how bad it was. No one except the Sorrow King, I guess."

"So, these Despair Minions, they work for the Sorrow King?" asked Ava.

Leo nodded. "Exactly."

"What do we do now, Leo?" Ava's eyes begged for guidance.

"We need to tell Santa what happened. If Christmas is to be saved, we're going to need more help."

"But isn't Santa at the North Pole? How are we going to get there?"

Leo grinned and said, "I know a way. I hope you're not afraid of caves."

Ava and Leo ran to the entrance of the Cave of Wonder, not realizing that they were following close behind the Sorrow King and the rest of his Despair Minions.

TWO DAYS BEFORE CHRISTMAS

S anta's castle glistened like a majestic winter wonderland under the shimmering moonlight. A warm fire crackled in the cozy workshop within the castle walls, filling the air with the scent of pine and joy. Santa and his hardworking elves were making toys and wrapping them in colorful paper, each one destined for the eager hands of deserving children on Christmas morning. The castle was overflowing with gifts awaiting their journey in Santa's magical sack.

With a hearty "Ho, ho, ho!" Santa chuckled as he surveyed the progress of his industrious elves. "Marvelous work, my little helpers. We may even finish ahead of schedule this year if we keep up this splendid pace!"

The elves rejoiced and hurried back to their duties. Santa's rosy nose crinkled with amusement as he added, "I must check on our beloved reindeer. Do not stop your work, my friends. I will return shortly."

Santa left his grand chair and headed for the reindeer stables outside the castle. There, standing proudly, were Dasher, Dancer, Prancer, Rudolph, Comet, Cupid, Donner, and Blitzen. But Vixen was nowhere in sight.

"Aha! Vixen, you mischievous little rascal. Where have you run off to?" He searched behind the stables, but there was no sign of Vixen. Curiosity led Santa along the perimeter of the castle walls to the training yard. A dark silhouette stood out against the radiant moonlight. Vixen stood at the far end of the training yard's wooden fence.

Santa clicked his tongue and yelled, "Vixen! Return to your stable. Rest is essential if you are to embark on our long journey tomorrow night!"

"I'm afraid her services won't be necessary, dear Santa Claus." A frigid gust of snow and ice swirled around, announcing the arrival of the Sorrow King.

Santa struggled to catch his breath, his chest burning from the icy onslaught. He gasped for air and prepared to face the threatening wizard. Santa was determined to protect the spirit of Christmas!

The Sorrow King looked at Santa Claus with a sinister grin. Then he commanded his horde of Despair Minions to attack the jolly old elf. Santa was overwhelmed before he could mount a defense.

"Why must you do this, Sorrow King?" Santa's voice rang out, his jolly voice now filled with sorrow. The Despair Minions grabbed Santa and held him tight.

"My dear Santa Claus," sneered the Sorrow King. "You know I thrive on the pain and suffering of others. After all, it was you and those old elves in the forest that banished me to the Dark Realm centuries ago. And now I have returned to settle the score."

"We banished you to the Dark Realm because you sought to steal all the Christmas Spirit from this world," said Santa.

"Give it up, Santa. You care so deeply for the human world; too bad they don't care about you anymore. They've lost the Christmas Spirit. Nothing you or your guardian elf can do will change that now."

"That's not true!" Santa's voice thundered, and with a wrinkle of his nose, Santa broke free from the grasp of the Despair Minions. "Now, Dasher! now, Dancer! now Prancer and Vixen! On, Comet! on, Cupid! on, Donner on Blitzen! Dash to me, Rudolph! Dash to me, all!"

The nine faithful reindeer rallied to the side of

their beloved master. Thousands of Despair Minions materialized, their presence seemingly endless.

The Sorrow King laughed with glee. "I can feel my powers growing stronger by the second. The Christmas Spirit is too weak to stop me now!"

A fierce battle erupted, Santa's warm laughter clashing with the Sorrow King's sinister cackles. Donner and Cupid stood by Santa's side as the Despair Minions swarmed them from every direction. Rudolph's nose blazed like embers in a fiery display. The Sorrow King fixed his gaze on Rudolph as his evil minions went after the others. With a mighty whinny, Rudolph galloped straight at the Sorrow King. His nose lit a path as he charged through the Despair Minions, tossing them aside with his massive antlers.

The Sorrow King raised his hands and sent waves of black shadows swirling toward Rudolph. The waves twisted and snaked through the air, but the brave reindeer managed to dodge the attack. Rudolph closed in on the Sorrow King, lowered his head, and slammed into the evil being. The collision sent the Sorrow King soaring through the air. But to Rudolph's horror, the Sorrow King manipulated the currents around him and came to a stop in midair. Hovering over the frozen ground, the Sorrow King moved his arms to the side, creating a force that knocked Rudolph to the ground. Nearby Despair Minions saw the fallen reindeer and trapped him.

With Rudolph now captured, the Sorrow King turned his attention to Santa Claus. "Had enough, Santa?"

"Do not underestimate the power of the Christmas Spirit, Sorrow King!" Santa's voice echoed. "It can bring light to even the darkest corners of the world."

The battle raged on, and Santa and his reindeer fought fearlessly against the forces of the Sorrow King. The air crackled with sparks of hope as the reindeer's hooves pounded against the frozen ground.

Santa's laughter and "Ho, ho, ho's" boomed like drums across the battlefield. His eyes burned bright as he called upon the ancient magic coursing through his body. Santa unleashed magical bolts of shimmering light with every wrinkle of his button nose. Each one repelled the oncoming horde of Despair Minions. But for every minion defeated, two more took its place.

"You will not prevail, Sorrow King!" Santa's voice rang out with authority. "Your darkness will not extinguish the spirit of Christmas!"

Despite their best efforts, one by one the reindeer fell to the Despair Minions. The evil powers of the Sorrow King were relentless. With each blow, Santa's strength diminished, and soon he was outmatched. The Sorrow

King's dark energy and the countless waves of Despair Minions overwhelmed Santa. The jolly old elf fell into the hands of his enemy.

The air hung heavy with defeat as Santa Claus and his reindeer stood before the Sorrow King. Their hopes flickered like dying embers as they were bound by shadowy chains, unable to escape.

Santa stared at the Sorrow King with a determined look, refusing to be consumed by despair.

"Sorrow King," he said. "What do you hope to accomplish?"

The Sorrow King sneered, his voice dripping with hate. "Santa Claus, you and your merry companions have brought joy and happiness to these realms for far too long. I have come to destroy the Christmas Spirit and plunge the world into eternal sorrow. And you, Santa, will bear witness to the ruin of your beloved holiday."

"You may have defeated us for now," said Santa, narrowing his eyes. "But the Christmas Spirit cannot be so easily erased. No matter what you do, it will endure."

The Sorrow King's laugh sent a shiver down Santa's spine. "Oh, Santa Claus, your optimism is admirable but foolish. I will banish you and your reindeer to the Dark Realm, where joy and light are but distant memories. There you will be forgotten, and your legacy will crumble."

Santa looked into the eyes of the Sorrow King. "Even in darkness, hope can be found," he said. "The Christmas Spirit will live on, for it is a beacon of love and joy that will never fade away."

The Sorrow King's expression twisted with rage. "Enough!" he thundered. "Your words will not save you. Prepare to say goodbye."

Santa turned to his faithful reindeer as the Sorrow King raised his arms and prepared to cast his banishing spell. They stood tall–ready to face whatever challenges awaited them in the Dark Realm.

Santa met the Sorrow King's gaze one last time. "Though you may send us away, Sorrow King, the Christmas spirit will endure. It will find a way to shine, even in the darkest of places."

With those words hanging in the air, the Sorrow King unleashed his dark magic. Santa and his reindeer became engulfed in a cloud of shadows. The Sorrow King released one last burst of power and banished Santa and his reindeer to the depths of the Dark Realm. Triumph flashed in the Sorrow King's eyes as his body began to transform. The imposing dark figure morphed into a jolly old elf dressed in red. The Sorrow King was now disguised as Santa Claus himself. A group of Despair

Minions twisted and turned their broken bodies into hideous reindeer-like figures. When their transformation was complete, they entered the empty stables.

Deep inside Santa's Castle, the elves continued their task in the workshop, oblivious to the fate of their beloved leader. Silently, the Sorrow King crept into Santa's workshop. Dressed in Santa's familiar red suit and sporting a fake white beard, he plotted his destruction of the Christmas Spirit.

JOURNEY TO SANTA'S CASTLE

A va's heart raced with excitement as they approached the entrance to the Cave of Wonder. They screeched to a halt as a blast of icy wind whipped past them, blowing Leo's green hat off his head.

"Oh no!" Leo exclaimed. "My hat! Here, hold on to this."

He handed Lumina to Ava, who grabbed the magic scepter and held it to her chest. Instantly, Lumina's crystal shard burst into a brilliant flood of light. Leo shielded his eyes from the intense glow in front of him.

"Um, Leo," Ava whispered. "What's happening?"

"This is amazing!" Leo exclaimed as he secured his hat

back on his head. "I've been training with Lumina for years, but I've never seen her glow like that."

Ava looked unsure.

"Should I give her back?"

A grin spread across Leo's face as he shook his head.

"No way! Lumina seems to have taken a liking to you, Ava. It appears you have a special bond with her."

Ava blushed and took a few steps forward.

"Let's get on with it then. Lead the way, Lumina!"

Thanks to Lumina's guiding light, Leo and Ava easily climbed down the rocky ledge that had caused Leo so much trouble earlier. They reached the bottom of the giant rock face in no time. Ava held up Lumina to reveal their surroundings. Jagged rock formations stretched to the ceiling of the rough and uneven cave walls. Stalactites hung from the rocky ceiling like nature's chandeliers suspended in mid-air. Small stones and pebbles covered the ground, worn smooth over centuries by the dripping water.

"This place is incredible, Leo!" exclaimed Ava. "I can't believe this cave has been right outside my town all this time!"

Leo touched the rough cave wall, feeling every crack and crevice as he walked. "You think this cave is special? Wait until you see Santa's castle. Oh, and Mrs. Claus's gingerbread cookies? They'd make Rudolph stay home on a foggy night!" Just the thought of those cookies made Leo's stomach growl.

"Ha ha, Leo!" Ava chuckled. "I can hear your stomach growling all the way over here!"

Another gust of icy wind blew through the cave, chilling Ava and Leo to the bone. The growling echoed off the walls as it grew louder.

"I don't think that's my stomach," Leo said as a Despair Minion emerged from the shadows, its glowing red eyes cutting through the dark. "Ava, look out!"

The creature lunged at Ava with lightning speed, its claws outstretched. Leo unsheathed Everblade and leaped forward. The sound of metal clashing against sharp claws rang through the cavern as Leo fought the Despair Minion.

"Leo, use this!" Ava threw Lumina at Leo. The light drained from its crystal as the magical scepter did cartwheels through the air. Leo followed its path and jumped off the cave wall toward the flying scepter. He grabbed the staff and landed on the ground seconds before darkness consumed the cave.

"Be gone, you miserable beast!" shouted Leo as a blast of ice shot from Lumina and struck the Despair Minion.

Silence filled the cave. Leo and Ava stared at their

attacker on the cold cave floor. Tiny pieces of the monster started to float in the air as its body disintegrated. Leo circled the vanishing creature and stood next to Ava. Then he handed Lumina to her. The cave lit up like the night sky on the Fourth of July.

"I thought we got rid of all those things back in town?" Ava asked as she caught her breath.

"Not all of them," Leo replied. "And if they made it to the Cave of Wonder, that means...Santa! Ava, we have to hurry!" He grabbed Ava's arm and pulled her along as they ran through a long passage that led them into the Mystic Forest.

Elves frantically scurried about the workshop, wrapping gifts and placing bright green and red bows on top.

The Impostor Claus inspected the busy elves as they worked. He looked down at the table where a group of elves were wrapping presents.

"What's this?" he said, picking up a bright red tennis racket.

"That's for John McNeill," an elf said. "He asked for a tennis racket for Christmas, remember?"

"Oh, of course," said Impostor Claus. He walked over

to another table and examined the toys there.

"These are sure to be a hit this year," said Impostor Claus. He reached down and examined a pair of Giggle Goggles. "How do they work?"

"Just put them on and press the little button on the side," said another elf.

Impostor Claus slowly put on the goggles and pressed the button. He immediately burst out laughing, unable to control himself. The elves all stared and laughed with their fake Santa Claus as he struggled to remove the goggles.

"Get them–ha ha ha–off of me–ha ha ha!" he laughed. Impostor Claus shook his head until the goggles flew off. The room fell silent. "Destroy them. All of them. Now, back to work."

Mrs. Claus moved gracefully through the workshop as the elves went back to work. She carried a tray piled high with warm gingerbread cookies and a second tray stacked two feet high with steaming mugs of hot cocoa. The smell of sugary goodness drifted through the air with every step Mrs. Claus took.

Mrs. Claus smiled as she addressed the room full of busy elves. "Time for a little treat, my dear elves!" All the elves stopped in their tracks. Their eyes widened with delight like stars sparkling in the sky. They gathered around the table where Mrs. Claus had placed the trays stacked high with cookies and hot cocoa. One by one, the elves reached for the treats. Their mouths watered as they savored each bite and sip. Everyone in the workshop was enjoying their well-deserved break. Everyone, that is, except Santa Claus. Mrs. Claus scanned the room for her companion and found him tucked away in a shadowy corner.

"Wouldn't you like some treats, Mr. Claus?" she asked.

A mischievous smile formed on the face of Impostor Claus as he approached Mrs. Claus. His eyes burned with mystery. "Dear Mrs. Claus, your kindness and generosity are truly remarkable," he complimented with an eerie sweetness. Mrs. Claus studied the jolly old elf as he crossed the room. She sensed something different about Santa but couldn't put her finger on it.

"Thank you, Mr. Claus. The elves looked exhausted from all their hard work. Don't you think they deserve a treat every now and then?" she asked with a hint of suspicion.

"As a matter of fact, they do," he said. "They have done so much to prepare for our big night tomorrow. But I do have one special request from our most helpful friends."

The elves paused in their enjoyment of cookies and cocoa to hear the impostor's proposal. It was very unlike Santa to make special requests so close to Christmas.

Impostor Claus continued, "What if we could harness

the power of the Christmas Spirit in an...extraordinary way?" He leaned closer to Mrs. Claus. "What if we built a machine that could amplify the Christmas Spirit to levels the world has never known?"

Santa's wild suggestion sent a shiver down her spine.

"What do you mean, Mr. Claus?" she asked "How can we amplify the Christmas Spirit?"

Impostor Claus paced around the room, making wild gestures as he described his plan.

"When I make my journey tomorrow eve, my machine will take the Christmas Spirit from every good boy and girl I visit. Then, it will take that collective Christmas Spirit and unleash a great wave of joy and magic upon the world!" His words echoed off the walls of the workshop with glee.

A great sense of unease settled over the room like a thick fog as the impostor laid out his plan. Mrs. Claus's heart raced as she listened. She knew that tampering with the delicate balance of the Christmas Spirit was a dangerous game to play.

"Santa, the Christmas Spirit is precious, as you know best," she said. "Altering it may have unintended consequences."

The impostor nodded.

"You are absolutely right, dear Mrs. Claus. We will be

very careful. But if all goes according to plan, the power of the Christmas Spirit will be unstoppable!"

Ava and Leo adjusted their eyes to the soft light of the Mystic Forest as they left the Cave of Wonder. The crisp air carried the sweet scent of pine and the whispers of the trees.

"Wow, Leo! Look at this place!" Ava said, and her eyes grew wide with wonder. "It's like stepping into a magical dream."

Leo grinned. "Welcome to the Mystic Forest, Ava. The path through these trees will lead us straight to Santa's castle."

They ran hand in hand, their footsteps landing softly on the white ground. Their breath formed tiny clouds in the crisp air. Leaves began to rustle, and a gentle breeze whispered past them. The forest came alive as Leo and Ava made their way down the winding path of glowing flowers. She thought the flowers looked like tiny stars scattered along the path.

"Leo, look at these flowers!" Ava exclaimed. "They're like little bursts of magic lighting our way."

A grin spread across his face. "They are magical, Ava.

Just like you."

Ava's cheeks blushed at the compliment. She was grateful to have Leo as her companion. His words of encouragement lifted her spirits.

"Leo, can you tell me about Santa Claus?" Ava asked.

"What would you like to know?" he replied.

"Well, is he nice?"

"Of course he's nice! He's the nicest, jolliest elf you'll ever meet!"

"What about Mrs. Claus? Are her gingerbread cookies really as good as you say they are?"

"They're the tastiest gingerbread cookies in the world. Warm and chewy. She always has a fresh batch in the oven just in case we elves get hungry. Oh, and they're so sweet, too. Mrs. Claus always puts lots of honey in each batch. In fact, she uses so much honey, you have to drink two cups of hot cocoa to wash the sweetness down."

The wind blew clouds of snow from the tops of the great evergreens all around them. It was as if the forest itself was trying to speak, whispering secrets of the unknown before them.

"Leo, do you feel it?" asked Ava, her voice full of wonder. "The forest seems to be alive. Like it's urging us on."

Leo nodded. "Yes, Ava. The forest knows we're on a

mission and is leading us to where we need to be. That feeling will only get stronger the closer we get to Santa's castle."

A voice called out from a nearby grove as the two picked up their pace. "Leo," it beckoned. "We have something important to tell you."

Leo skidded to a halt, startled by the sound. He turned and saw the wise and ancient faces of the Elder Elves standing in the shade of the great evergreens. She tugged at Leo's arm, urging him to keep running, but Leo remained put. His eyes darted between Ava and the elves.

"I'm sorry, Elder Elves, but we're in a hurry. I think Santa needs our help."

The Elders looked at each other. Then they turned to Leo. "Farewell, Leo. We'll see you soon." They watched in silence as Leo and Ava sprinted past.

"Do you believe we should have stopped them?" Elder Willowbloom asked.

Elder Oakbranch thought for a moment before answering, "No, my friend. Sometimes, it's in the journey that one discovers the answers they seek. Let Leo find his own way and learn the lessons that await him."

Once they were out of sight, Ava asked Leo, "Who were those people?"

"They were the Elder Elves," replied Leo. "They are the

defenders of the Mystic Forest. They helped me find the cave that led me to you."

"So they're not dangerous?" asked Ava.

"Not at all. You see, long ago, Santa Claus and the Elder Elves saved Christmas—the world, really—from the Sorrow King. They banished him and his minions to this place called the Dark Realm."

Ava listened as Leo explained the history of the Elder Elves and their importance in his world. Knowing that other powerful warriors were in the fight against the Sorrow King reassured her.

Ava and Leo could see the path opening past the trees ahead of them. They had reached the edge of the Mystic Forest and were one step closer to the heart of the North Pole. Yet, the sky above them turned a deep black as if someone had pulled a blanket over the moon and stars.

Rolling hills of pristine white snow stretched past the trees and the glowing flowers. In the distance, towering cliffs disappeared into the dark sky. Atop the largest hill stood Santa's majestic castle.

"There it is," said Leo. "Santa's castle. The heart of all Christmas magic."

Ava's eyes widened in wonder as she took in the panoramic view. "Leo, it really is like a winter wonderland! Do you think Santa and his elves are okay?"

"I'm not sure. I don't see any signs of the Sorrow King or his Despair Minions."

"Maybe that one in the cave just ran away during the fight and thought it was a good place to hide?" Ava wondered aloud.

"I suppose that's possible," said Leo. "We haven't seen any others since, and even the Elder Elves didn't warn us about the Despair Minions or the Sorrow King."

Leo and his Ava approached the castle, climbing the hill towards the stables. As they got closer, Leo's attention was drawn to the reindeer.

"That's odd," said Leo.

"What's that?" asked Ava.

"The reindeer...they look...I don't know, something's off."

Ava followed Leo's gaze, her eyes widening with curiosity. "What do you mean, Leo? They look like ordinary reindeer to me."

"It's their antlers," said Leo. "They look like skeletons growing out of the reindeer's heads."

"It's too dark out here, Leo," said Ava. "I can't see very well."

Leo thought for a moment and shook his head. "You're probably right. It must be the trickery of the shadows." He shrugged the thought out of his head. "We're so close to

Santa's castle. Come on, let's keep going."

Finally, they reached the magnificent doors of Santa's castle.

"Welcome to Santa Claus's castle," Leo said. He pushed open the large wooden doors.

Ava took a deep breath. She wasn't sure if she was prepared for the world of magic and wonder that awaited inside. Their fingers intertwined as she took Leo's hand. Together they stepped through the grand entrance.

IMPOSTOR CLAUS

An orchestra of tinkering and clattering filled the air of Santa's workshop. The hard-working elves used their small hands to piece together the complex parts of the Christmas Spirit amplifying machine.

Impostor Claus's voice boomed through the workshop, "Faster! Not there! Don't you understand the importance of the Christmas Spirit? Move, move, move! Christmas Eve is approaching at an alarming rate!" His sharp commands shook the elves from their concentration.

The workshop floor was covered with bits of metal, screws, and wires. In the center of the workshop stood an impressive contraption designed by the castle's brightest minds. It was a large metal box decorated with a collection of colorful buttons and finely tuned dials.

At the top of the machine was a large horn, its design resembling that of an antique record player. The horn had been added to capture the Christmas Spirit and draw it into the metal box below. Despite Impostor Claus's barking orders, every turn of a screw and connection of a wire was completed with precision and care.

Mrs. Claus bustled about the kitchen. She had to make sure a constant supply of hot cocoa was ready for the hard-working elves. But her eyes were not just on the delicious treats. She couldn't shake the feeling that something was different about her dear Santa. Even with Christmas Eve just around the corner, she had never seen him act this way. Santa was always a cheerful elf, eating cookies and drinking hot cocoa, even during the busiest times of the year. He appeared anxious, a far cry from his usual jolly personality.

The workshop erupted in excitement as she pulled a fresh batch of cookies from the oven. Mrs. Claus darted for the door, almost dropping the tray. She was relieved to see Leo standing tall among the other elves. They had surrounded Leo with smiling faces.

Leo was bombarded from all sides with praise and questions from the other elves.

"Leo! You're back!" exclaimed one elf, unable to contain his excitement.

"It's good to see you again!" chimed in another.

Amidst the crowd of voices, Leo tried his best to answer their questions.

"I'm happy to be back here in Santa's castle," he said with a grin.

But before he could share the details of his journey, an eager voice asked, "Who is your new friend?"

Leo turned to face the curious elf then his eyes shifted to Ava standing by his side. He grinned from pointy ear to pointy ear as he introduced her to the bustling crowd.

"Everyone, this is Ava. She's my brave companion I met in the Human Realm. Together we saved the Christmas Spirit in her town."

"Hello!" Ava said. She could hardly believe that she was standing in Santa's workshop talking to his elves.

"Oh, Leo," said Mrs. Claus. She approached the tired pair with the tray of gingerbread cookies still steaming from the oven. "It is so good to see you again. I'm sure you both must be exhausted from your travels. Would you like a cookie?"

Ava's eyes widened as she reached for the tray, but she stopped when Leo said, "No time, Mrs. Claus. We need to speak with Santa. It's very important."

They searched the room for the jolly old elf, but he was nowhere to be found.

"How strange," said Mrs. Claus. "He was just here. I wonder where he went?"

"We'll find him, Mrs. Claus," said Leo.

"When you do, please find out what's bothering him," said Mrs. Claus. "He's barely touched his hot cocoa all day. And he hasn't taken a single bite of my gingerbread cookies since you left."

Leo's grin turned to a frown when his eyes caught sight of the metal box and oversized horn in the center of the workshop. He walked over to the machine and studied it, touching every button and switch.

"What's this?" asked Leo. An eager elf stepped forward, ready to explain.

"Santa asked us to build it," the elf said. "It's a machine he wants to use on his journey tomorrow night. He's going to collect all the Christmas Spirit in the world and amplify its power. He said he wants to spread even more joy and happiness."

There was something about the machine that didn't sit right with Leo.

"Are you sure this is what Santa wants?" he asked. "Altering the Christmas Spirit on such a grand scale...it feels like a risk."

Mrs. Claus circled the machine.

"Leo, dear, I share your concern," she confessed. "The

Christmas Spirit is a delicate being, and tampering with it may have unintended consequences. I fear altering it this way may do more harm than good."

"We need to find out what's really going on," said Leo. "Are you coming, Mrs. Claus?"

"Oh, I better go tend to the elves and their treats," said Mrs. Claus. "You know how hungry they get this time of year."

Ava was still eyeing the gingerbread cookies on Mrs. Claus's tray when Leo said, "Come on, Ava. Let's go find Santa."

The two of them navigated through rows of busy elves as they made their way through the workshop. They ran through a side door and up the staircase which led to the very top of Santa's castle. The large wooden steps creaked as they climbed each one.

The landing opened up to a long hallway decorated with twinkling lights and festive garlands. At the far end was the biggest Christmas tree Ava had ever seen. Its branches were covered with colorful ornaments and shimmering lights that danced from the trunk to the top. Ava couldn't help but gasp at its beauty. Leo's keen elf ears picked up a faint sound coming from one of the adjacent rooms.

"Over there," Leo whispered, pointing to an ajar door across the hall. "I think I heard something."

Together they approached the door, holding their breath in anticipation. Leo creaked the door open, revealing a dimly lit room. Sitting near the fireplace was Santa Claus, his shoulders slumped.

"Santa," Leo whispered as he entered the room. "I have returned from my journey!"

Impostor Claus remained silent, staring at the dancing flames before him. Ava entered the room and stood next to Leo.

"Santa, are you okay?" asked Leo.

"Ho ho ho," muttered Impostor Claus. "Glad to see you arrived in one piece."

"We've been looking all over for you," Leo said. "I did what you asked. I talked to the Elder Elves, and they sent me through the Cave of Wonder. I found the Human Realm and my new friend, Ava. Together we brought the Christmas Spirit back to her town—"

"—But then I was attacked by those horrible Despair Minions," interjected Ava. "And...and Leo saved me. But it wasn't easy—"

"We need your help, Santa."

Impostor Claus rose from his chair and turned to face Ava and Leo. He smiled and spoke with a mysterious voice. "My dear children, I understand your concern. The Sorrow King and his Despair Minions are indeed powerful

76

foes. But fear not, for I have a plan."

Leo glanced at Ava and said, "What plan, Santa? Does it have something to do with that machine the elves are building? That thing doesn't look safe."

"That machine is essential to our cause," said Impostor Claus. "It will amplify the Christmas Spirit, spreading joy and happiness like never before."

"But something doesn't feel right, Santa," said Ava, voicing her concern. "That machine looks dangerous. Are you sure it's for the greater good?"

Ava and Leo stood frozen, their eyes glued to Impostor Claus as he paced back and forth. Impostor Claus paused in front of the fireplace, his silhouette shrouding the two friends in darkness.

He let out a deep sigh and said, "My dear Ava, doubt can cloud even the brightest minds. Believe me, the machine is necessary if we plan on restoring the true magic of Christmas. That machine will give hope to those who have lost it."

Impostor Claus settled back into his seat, a faint smile playing on his lips. He looked at Ava and Leo and said, "Now, my dear friends, it is time to rest. A monumental task awaits us tomorrow night. The fate of Christmas rests on our shoulders."

CHRISTMAS EVE

L eo tossed and turned in his bed. The events in the castle earlier had left him feeling unsettled. The pitch-black sky outside didn't help to calm his nerves. The clouds would reveal a sliver of moonlight even on the snowiest nights at the North Pole. But on this night, darkness clung to the world like a cloak of shadows, enveloping everything in its inky embrace.

Mrs. Claus's words echoed in Leo's mind. *Something was definitely wrong with Santa Claus. Building a machine to amplify the Christmas Spirit?* Questions raced through Leo's mind the more he thought about Santa's creation. In all the years he had known Santa, Leo had never heard him ask the elves to build something for himself. Leo knew he had to find out the truth.

He slipped out of bed past Ava, who was fast asleep on the floor next to him. He tiptoed through the silent corridors of the castle like a shadow, aware of every creaking board beneath his feet. His sharp eyes scanned the halls for any sign of Santa, but the jolly old elf was nowhere to be found. Leo's mind was a whirlwind of confusion and worry, tugging at his emotions.

His breath caught in his throat as he entered the workshop. The room should have been alive with the vibrant energy of toy-making elves. Instead, it was empty, free of the elves' joyful hustle and bustle. Leo's eyes widened in disbelief. *Where had all the toys gone? And the mysterious machine?* thought Leo. It was as if an invisible hand had swept away everything that made up the workshop. Leo knew he had to keep searching, to delve deeper into the castle's depths.

Step by cautious step, Leo descended farther down the corridors. The castle was unusually quiet, like a silent sleeping giant. He saw none of the familiar faces of his fellow elves. Their absence added to the growing mystery that consumed Leo's thoughts. It felt strange—deeply strange—for the castle to be so empty. So devoid of the usual preparations for Santa's great journey.

Leo creaked open the door to Santa's study and entered the room. He scanned the area for any signs of activity.

He noticed the faint glow of dying embers in the fireplace. *Someone was here not long ago,* thought Leo. His elf ears strained to pick up any sound, any sign of life.

Then, from beneath the floor, a faint sound reached Leo's ears. It was soft, rhythmic breathing that tickled his curiosity. His eyes darted around, searching for a clue to the source of the mysterious sound. Leo stamped his feet once. Then he did it again. A voice from below shouted, "Stop! You're getting dirt in our eyes."

Leo froze like a statue.

"Who said that?" said Leo.

"I did!" the voice shouted again. Then there was a thud on the floor under the green rug in the middle of the study. Leo lifted the rug only to discover a hidden trap door. His hands trembled as he lifted the door, revealing a vast secret chamber. Shock washed over Leo as he gasped at the sight before him. His fellow elves were trapped and hidden beneath the floor of Santa's study!

"What are you all doing here?" asked Leo. "Why are you hiding under the floor of Santa's study?"

The elves looked at each other uneasily before one of them spoke up.

"Santa put us here!" he exclaimed.

"Yeah, he told us our services were no longer required," said another.

"What happened to all the toys in the workshop?" Leo asked, hoping for a reasonable explanation.

"Well, we threw them away, of course," an elf replied matter-of-factly.

"Threw them away?!" Leo exclaimed in disbelief. "But tomorrow is Christmas. Why would you throw away the presents for all the good boys and girls?"

"...Santa said they weren't necessary this year," muttered one elf. "He said the real gift would come later when he had all the Christmas Spirit of the world."

"What did Santa have you do with the machine?" asked Leo.

"We attached it to his sleigh," chimed in another elf.

Leo was dumbfounded by what the elves had just told him.

"Come on, get out from under the floor," Leo urged, motioning for the elves to join him.

"That's okay," said one elf. "Santa told us to stay down here no matter what. And that's what we're going to do."

Leo shook his head in frustration.

"Fine. Do you know where Santa is right now?"

"He's about to embark on his journey to the Human Realm!" the elves said.

"But it's too early for that. Santa never leaves before breakfast..." Then it hit Leo like a bolt of lightning. The

Despair Minion in the cave. The Elder Elves trying to talk to him in the Mystic Forest. The strange-looking reindeer outside. Santa Claus refusing to eat Mrs. Claus's gingerbread cookies. The elves trapped under the floor.

"The machine," Leo whispered.

"Leo? Are you in here?" a voice said from outside Santa's study. It was Ava.

"Ava! How did you know I was here?" asked Leo.

"I saw you get up and tiptoe out of your room. You looked suspicious, so I followed you around the castle."

"We have to go. Right now. We have to stop Santa before it's too late."

"Stop him from what?" asked Ava.

"From destroying Christmas!"

Hidden beneath the cover of the darkened sky, the Sorrow King plotted his escape. He shed his Santa Claus disguise and revealed his true form. With an evil grin etched on his face, he stood like a menacing shadow over Santa's bright red sleigh. The unsuspecting elves had anchored the Christmas Spirit amplifying machine to the back of the sleigh.

The night was thick with the Sorrow King's evil, and

even nature seemed to recoil in fear. His nine loyal Despair Minions waited for his command, each ready to pounce like a pack of hungry wolves. They yipped and growled as he approached the stables, their red eyes glowing in anticipation of their journey.

"The time has come, dear friends," the Sorrow King said. "Soon, our reign will spread across these lands. But first, we must pay a visit to our friends in the Human Realm." With the turn of a key, the stables' doors swung open, releasing his minions into the night. Like bolts of lightning, they raced to claim their positions at the front of Santa's sleigh.

The Sorrow King marveled at the sight before him. His twisted, reindeer-like minions were eager to pull Santa's famous red sleigh. The famous red sleigh of joy and happiness—now a machine of misery. And to top it off, he did it all right in front of the elves, Mrs. Claus, and Santa's guardian elf.

He climbed into the back of the sleigh and took the reins. With a quick sweep of his arms, he whipped the Despair Minions into motion. The sleigh, the Sorrow King, and the machine took off into the night sky, heading straight for the Human Realm.

The large wooden doors to the castle wouldn't budge an inch. Leo pushed again. Ava helped this time, but the doors remained closed.

"The Sorrow King must have blocked the doors from the outside," said Leo.

"The Sorrow King? He's here?"

"He's been Santa this whole time! I don't know how he did it, or what he did to the real Santa Claus. But I know it's him."

"Then we have to stop him! Isn't there another way we can get outside?"

"There are other doors, sure. But they're probably blocked as well. I have an idea. Stand back, Ava!"

Leo grabbed Lumina and raised her with both hands. With all his might, he cast a blinding ball of light that blew apart the wooden doors. A cascade of splinters and debris scattered around them. When the dust settled and their eyes adjusted, Ava and Leo saw what had blocked the door. It was thousands of beautifully wrapped presents. The Sorrow King had taken the gifts the elves had made and piled them up ten stacks high.

They pushed through piles of baby dolls, roller skates,

and toy trucks. What should have been gifts for the good boys and girls of the world were now being used as a barricade to stop Leo. Once they cleared the wall of toys, Ava and Leo turned left and headed straight for the reindeer's stables.

The snow-covered ground was frozen. Ava and Leo struggled to find their footing on the icy ground as they rounded the castle wall. Leo scanned the landscape ahead, looking for any sign of the Sorrow King. He saw the stable doors hanging wide open but there were no reindeer inside.

"Look at all those marks on the ground," Ava said. Two long and deep gashes, about four feet apart, were carved into the icy snow. Leading away from the lines were dozens of small circular marks. "And here, these look like hoof prints!"

"Those two gashes are from the tracks of Santa's sleigh," said Leo. "And those hoof prints are from the reindeer. We're too late, Ava. The Sorrow King is gone."

"What do we do, Leo?"

"Let me think."

How do we stop him from stealing the Christmas Spirit? Who would know where Santa is? thought Leo. Only one thing came to Leo's mind. *The Elder Elves.*

"We have to go back to the Mystic Forest," said Leo. He

85

pointed to the magnificent evergreen trees in the distance. Leo couldn't believe he had been so careless in ignoring the Elder Elves earlier. Now he understood the importance of their message. He had missed his chance to stop the Sorrow King from stealing the Christmas Spirit.

"The Elder Elves... They tried to tell me something before, and I ignored them. I was too caught up trying to get back to Santa's castle when I should have listened to what they had to say."

"Don't be too hard on yourself, Leo," said Ava. She placed her arm on Leo's shoulder and pulled him close. "Your intentions were pure. You just wanted to help Santa."

"You don't understand," said Leo. "I am Santa's guardian elf. I'm supposed to protect Santa from danger...and I failed him. Now the Sorrow King has taken his sleigh and his reindeer. He's going to win, Ava."

Ava grabbed Leo's shoulders and turned him so they were face-to-face. She squeezed the guardian elf's hands tight and said, "Then make it right. Let's go rescue Santa and save the Christmas Spirit."

Leo's bright blue eyes locked with Ava's deep green eyes. He grinned and pulled Lumina from his belt. For a moment, he admired the beauty of his magical scepter. Then he handed it to Ava without hesitation.

"You'll need this where we're going. Come on, let's go get our jolly old elf."

They raced through the darkness down the hill from Santa's castle and straight into the Mystic Forest.

The Sorrow King checked Santa's list and found his next victim's name.

Timothy Daniels: New bicycle. 21 speeds. Black with flames.

Timothy dreamed of the brand-new bicycle he so desperately wanted. Twenty-one speeds. A black frame with red and orange flames going up to the handlebars. He knew the bicycle would be too big for him at first. But in a few months, he would grow into it and tear down the streets of his small town. Santa Claus had assured him that the bicycle would be waiting for him on Christmas morning. Timothy knew it would be there, between the fireplace and the Christmas tree in his living room.

Santa's sleigh crashed hard on the roof of Timothy's house. The Despair Minions were far more careless than the real reindeer had ever been.

He chuckled. "No new bicycle for you this year, dear Timothy. How about a dictionary and a box of markers as dry as the desert sand?"

The Sorrow King flicked his wrist and summoned his dark magic, sending the tainted gifts tumbling down the chimney. They looked like withered shadows, covered in soot and ash, as they landed in the living room below.

The Sorrow King turned one dial on his machine. The Despair Minions broke into a wicked dance as the machine hummed with power. A dim white light of Christmas Spirit shimmered from the heart of Timothy. The little bit of Christmas Spirit bounced over his body for a few seconds, like a fly trying to escape the clutches of a spider's web. Suddenly, the machine on Santa's sleigh sucked in the light and trapped it inside.

A cloud of darkness trailed behind the Sorrow King and his minions like a suffocating shroud. The jagged gears of the machine atop Santa's sleigh whirred and clanked. It sucked up the remaining Christmas Spirit with a greedy hunger as they rode from house to house, leaving behind a barren wasteland of gloom. Like a cruel artist, the Sorrow King painted the world in darkness, removing the light of hope and leaving a trail of sorrow in his wake.

THE DARK REALM

A va and Leo were caught in a blinding snowstorm as they raced through the Mystic Forest. The pair had to shield their eyes from the stinging snow to keep up their frantic pace. The wind howled through the tall evergreen trees, sending many of the old ones crashing to the ground. Leo jumped over fallen branches and rolled under huge logs that blocked their path. Ava struggled to keep up with the nimble elf.

They ventured farther into the forest and came to the clearing where Leo first encountered the Elder Elves. One by one, the elves stepped from behind the giant evergreen tree. Ava thought they looked like ghosts moving in a thick fog. The Elder Elves formed a circle around Ava and Leo.

"Leo," said Elder Willowbloom. "Are you ready to speak

with us now?"

Leo hung his head low. "Yes, I am ready."

"Good. We elves have seen the unfolding of these dark times. You now know that the Sorrow King infiltrated Santa's castle and stole his identity. And now he is well on his way to rid the world of the Christmas Spirit."

"What has he done to Santa Claus?" asked Leo.

"The Sorrow King sent Santa Claus and the reindeer into the treacherous depths of the Dark Realm," said Elder Oakbranch.

Tears formed in the corners of Leo's eye at the news. "Can we save him? Can we bring Santa back to the North Pole?"

The Elder Elves looked at each other. "There is a way, young Leo," said Elder Oakbranch. "In your hands is the key to Santa's salvation. The stone you found in the Cave of Wonder has the power to connect our realms. But it will only work if the Christmas Spirit is restored."

"So the stone won't work right now because the Sorrow King is stealing the Christmas Spirit?" asked Ava.

"Exactly," said Elder Oakbranch.

"So let's go stop him!" said Ava.

"You two cannot face him alone," said Elder Willowbloom. "Santa must be saved first if the Sorrow King is to be stopped."

"Then how do we enter the Dark Realm?" asked Leo.

"We have the power to send you there," said Elder Willowbloom. "Our magic can open a portal to the Dark Realm. We can only do this once, so it will be up to you to find Santa and then work to restore the Christmas Spirit. But take caution, for the Dark Realm is a dangerous place. We can see many things yet we can not see the threats that await you once you leave this place."

Leo clenched his fists. "We will do whatever it takes to stop the Sorrow King and bring Santa back home. Send us to the Dark Realm."

"Very well, Guardian Elf," said Elder Oakbranch. "Trust in your courage, believe in the light within your hearts, and use the power of the stone."

Ava and Leo took a deep breath while the Elder Elves began their mystical chant. A gust of wind sent snow swirling through the air, creating a tornado that reached high in the night sky. Ava winced and covered her ears as she tried to block the intense noise. Trees moaned and crashed to the ground with a thud.

Leo grabbed the handle of Everblade and braced himself. The Elder Elves continued their chant, summoning a brilliant flash of light. One moment Ava and Leo were standing in the Mystic Forest, and the next, they were standing in darkness.

91

The chant had worked. The Elder Elves had transported Ava and Leo into the mysterious Dark Realm.

"'Twas the night before Christmas, and all through the sky, the Sorrow King flew, whisking the Christmas Spirit goodbye," rhymed the Sorrow King. "The children all cried as I stole their joy from within, and kept it for myself, for it was time for my dark reign to begin!" He let out a sinister laugh as he finished his rendition.

The Christmas Spirit from millions of children had fallen victim to the Sorrow King. Their cries of sadness filled the night air as the Sorrow King rode to every corner of the globe. Soon the sun would begin to rise over the horizon and signal the beginning of Christmas Day.

"We must hurry, my loyal minions," said the Sorrow King. "The first light of dawn approaches, and we have yet to complete our mission. Only a few stops remain before we drain all the Christmas Spirit from this world."

The Despair Minions increased their pace. They raced against the coming sunrise, their hooves thundering against the sky.

"The long night will soon be over," said the Sorrow King. "Then we will retreat to my fortress and bask in the glorious embrace of eternal darkness!"

Ava held Lumina high above her head, but the darkness proved too strong for any light to shine. There were no stars or moon in the sky, only thick black clouds passed overhead, casting an eerie canopy across the land.

The ground beneath their feet was deep purple and was covered with jagged rocks and dried grass. Twisted trees stood barren, their branches reaching out like skeletal fingers. The path ahead shifted and rolled as shadows danced and flickered across the uneven terrain. Frozen grass and vegetation crunched beneath their feet as they moved forward. The air carried a chilly breeze, sending a shiver down Ava's spine.

Leo gripped Everblade in his right hand, ready to strike at the first sign of danger.

"Santa Claus!" Leo shouted. "Are you there?"

There was no answer. He tried again.

"Father Christmas! Where are you?"

Still no answer.

"Kris Kringle!" Leo shouted, then chuckled. "He hates that name."

"Let me try," said Ava. "Santa Claus? Saint Nicholas?

Can you hear me?" But there was no response.

Ava and Leo continued through the darkness of the Dark Realm. Their eyes scanned the shadows for any sign of Santa Claus. In the distance, a glimmer caught Leo's attention—a red glow piercing through the black.

"Ava, look," Leo whispered. He pointed forward, then gripped the handle of Everblade with both hands. "Despair Minion, straight ahead."

They crept toward the glow, not making a sound. The creature remained motionless on the frozen ground, unaware of Ava and Leo's approach. Leo held Everblade high above his head, waiting for the attack. Ava stood directly behind Leo. She hoped Lumina trusted her enough to help protect Leo if things got ugly.

The two were now within a few feet of the creature. They couldn't believe they had gotten so close without the minion noticing. Leo was seconds away from striking when he noticed the red glow was coming from the creature's nose.

"Wait, Rudolph?" asked Leo. "Is that really you?"

Rudolph raised his head and looked at Leo. The red-nosed reindeer jumped up and pranced around on the frozen ground. He snorted and huffed, unable to contain his excitement at seeing his old friend. Though he could not speak, his actions were enough.

"Oh, Rudolph!" cried Leo. He wrapped his arms around the neck of his old friend. "I can't believe we found you! Do you know where Santa is?" The reindeer lowered his head and nudged Ava and Leo, urging them to follow.

Rudolph led the way with his red nose lighting their path like a guiding star. Shadows bounced around every corner, trying to discourage them. But the light from Rudolph's nose helped calm their nerves.

Leo kept calling Santa's name. The longer they walked without seeing any sign of the jolly old elf, the more desperate his calls became. Ava was tired from the long journey. Her legs felt like jelly, and each step became more challenging than the last.

"Leo, I need to rest," said Ava. "I can't go any farther."

"We can't stop now," said Leo. "We have to find Santa and stop the Sorrow King."

Rudolph turned to Ava and recognized the pain in her voice. He knelt down and put his head between her legs, then used his great strength to lift Ava onto his back.

"Are you sure about this, Rudolph?" asked Ava. "I'm a lot heavier than the elves in Santa's castle!"

Rudolph let out a cheerful whinny and pranced onward. Ava held tightly to the harness tied around the reindeer's chest. Her whole body bounced in rhythm with Rudolph's every step. Ava felt calm sitting high on the reindeer's back, despite the darkness and creeping shadows. They searched desperately for Santa Claus, hoping to find any sign of the jolly elf.

Dawn had begun to break on the other side of the world. Thousands of children had woken up and wandered towards their family's Christmas tree. Beneath the trees sat lumps of coal and broken ornaments, dried markers and roller skates with only one wheel, misshapen teddy bears with missing eyes and arms, piles of wriggling worms, and broken alarm clocks. The twisted gifts left behind by the Sorrow King filled every child's heart with misery.

The Despair Minions guided Santa's sleigh to its final stop, where the machine sucked up the last of the Christmas Spirit.

"Santa and the rest of these elves will never forget the day they decided to cross my path," laughed the Sorrow King. "With all of the Christmas Spirit in my possession, these lands are now ours. You have done a marvelous job, my friends. Let us go home and celebrate!"

The Despair Minions unleashed a tremendous howl that echoed throughout the small town. Weary residents awoke from their slumber, drowning in sadness. The

Sorrow King pulled the reins hard and directed the minions toward the sky.

His mission was complete. The Sorrow King had drained the Christmas Spirit from the Human Realm, marking the beginning of his dark reign.

THE BATTLE FOR THE CHRISTMAS SPIRIT

- -

A chilling silence fell over the Dark Realm. The shadows stopped their evil dance across the frozen ground, and the cold wind came to a sudden halt.

"Something has changed," said Ava. "I can feel it all around me."

"We're too late," said Leo. "The Sorrow King...he's taken the Christmas Spirit. I've failed Santa Claus."

Leo fell to the ground and wept. Rudolph trotted up beside the guardian elf with Ava still on his back. They leaned down beside their friend and curled up beside him.

The three companions laid on the frozen ground in

defeat. They were at a loss for what to do next. The Sorrow King had bested them every step of the way. They felt hopeless and doomed to remain in this dreadful place forever.

Ava could feel a fiery light burning beside her. She lifted her head for a moment and looked at Lumina. But the crystal shard on the scepter was lifeless. Then she realized that Rudolph's nose was the source of the blazing light.

"Leo, look!" she exclaimed.

Leo turned his head and opened his eyes. His face lit up as he saw the red glow coming from the reindeer's nose.

Rudolph jumped to his feet and looked to his left. His eyes grew wide as he tilted his head. He resembled a dog listening to his master's call. Then Leo heard a voice calling from far away. Even though the darkness was too thick to see who was speaking, Leo still recognized that voice.

"Santa!" cried Leo. Rudolph lifted Ava onto his back again, and the three of them took off, following Santa's call.

Rudolph galloped at full speed with Leo at his side, the little elf running faster than even he thought possible.

"Rudolph!" they heard Santa call. "Where are you?"

Santa's voice grew louder as the three friends started up a steep hill.

"Santa!" yelled Leo. "Here we are!"

Santa Claus and the other reindeer came into view as Leo, Rudolph, and Ava reached the top of the hill. Santa and Leo ran into each other's arms and remained in their embrace for minutes as they cried tears of joy. Rudolph pranced and jumped with the other reindeer, nearly throwing Ava off his back during the celebration.

"Ho, ho, ho, Leo," chuckled Santa Claus. "How did you manage to get lost here in the Dark Realm?"

"The Elder Elves sent me—us—here," said Leo. "This is my friend, Ava. She's from the Human Realm. She's been helping me all this whole time."

"You brought a human into the Dark Realm?" asked Santa. "This is no place for a human!"

"It's okay, Santa," said Ava. "I would do anything to help you and save Christmas. Plus, I'm a huge fan."

"That's very sweet of you," said Santa. "But I'm afraid it's too late to save Christmas, dear Ava."

"Did you feel it, too?" asked Leo.

"Aye, I did, my old friend," said Santa. "The whole universe felt it, even if they didn't understand it."

As Santa, Leo, and Ava stood together, sharing their grief, Leo's sharp eyes caught sight of some large object behind Santa.

"Santa, what's that?" he asked, pointing to the peculiar sight. Santa turned, his eyes widening in surprise.

"Oh, that," he said with a chuckle. "That's my sleigh if you want to call it that. I built it from the fallen trees here in the Dark Realm. I hoped to use it to escape this place. Unfortunately, I couldn't fly without Rudolph's guiding light."

Rudolph looked at the other reindeer and danced proudly, holding his nose to the sky.

"Here, come look at this," said Santa Claus. "I may be old, but these hands can still build something marvelous when they need to."

Ava and Leo moved closer to get a better look at Santa's creation. The makeshift sleigh was barely big enough to hold Santa. Twisted limbs and branches intertwined like the weave of a wicker basket. Santa had pulled dried strips of bark to hold the pieces together, but Leo knew they wouldn't hold under any amount of pressure.

"Santa, it's..." started Leo. "...It's awful. That thing wouldn't hold you for more than five minutes!"

Before Santa could respond, a gust of wind swept through the air. They all turned to the sky and saw a bright circle of light forming in the darkness. The Sorrow King emerged from the middle of the circle, flying through on Santa's stolen sleigh pulled by the Despair Minions. Santa's face twisted into a look of confusion and then concern.

"He's got my sleigh! After him!" Santa exclaimed.

Without hesitating, Santa, Leo, and Ava climbed into the makeshift sleigh. Santa grabbed the reins and yelled, "Now, Dasher! now, Dancer! now Prancer and Vixen! On, Comet! on, Cupid! on, Donner on Blitzen! Dash away, Rudolph! Dash away, all!" The makeshift sleigh picked up speed as they rode after the Sorrow King, the wind whipping past their faces.

The reindeer galloped at an incredible pace, closing the gap between them and the Sorrow King. Rudolph led the pack, his bright red nose shining brightly in the dark sky. The air echoed with heated exchanges as the adversaries hurled taunts and challenges back and forth.

"Give me back my sleigh, you evil beast!" Santa shouted.

The Sorrow King's face narrowed at the sight of Santa and the rest of the sleigh.

"You're too late, Santa!" The Sorrow King shouted back. "I have all your precious Christmas Spirit right here." He tapped the machine on the back of the sleigh. Then the Sorrow King yanked on the reins, propelling his Despair Minions forward.

"He's getting away!" yelled Ava. "Can't you make this thing go any faster?"

Leo and Santa looked down at the crooked, makeshift sleigh, then locked eyes and shook their heads.

"I don't think that's a good idea, Ava," said Leo.

"We've got to do something!" she said. Ava scanned the sky, searching for anything that might help them. A faint glow caught her attention as her eyes passed by her own hands. "Lumina."

Ava raised the magic scepter, hoping it still worked. Aiming directly at the Sorrow King, she fired a blast of ice at Santa's real sleigh. The ice flew off into the sky, far behind her target. The Despair Minions were moving far too fast! Ava corrected her aim, this time pointing Lumina ahead of the Despair Minions. A second blast of ice shot out from the crystal shard. She missed again, but this time, her shot was much closer.

There must be a better way, she thought. Then Ava remembered how fast Rudolph had gone earlier when they had followed the sound of Santa's voice. He was only carrying her, not pulling Santa or a sleigh and eight other reindeer. Ava climbed over Santa and Leo, then jumped from the wooden sleigh onto the closest reindeer–Vixen.

"What are you doing?" Leo yelled.

Ava looked back at the guardian elf and smiled. "Don't worry, I have a plan!"

She reached forward and grabbed Donner's tail. Then she pulled herself onto his back with all her strength.

"Ava, you're going to get hurt!" yelled Santa. "Get back

here this instant!"

Ava ignored the jolly old elf and climbed forward. She focused on Blitzen and launched herself at the reindeer. Her foot slipped in the leap, making her miss her target. Ava's hands slipped down Blitzen's back, but she managed to grab the side reins and held on with all her strength.

Her heart raced as she braced herself against the force of the wind speeding past her. Ava refused to let go and tightened her fingers around the reins as she held on for dear life.

Leo watched in horror as Ava swayed back and forth over the dark depths below. Summoning all his strength, he jumped from the makeshift sleigh and landed on Blitzen. As soon as Leo regained his balance, he leaned over and grabbed Ava's hands that were gripping the reins. With a quick tug, he pulled Ava to safety.

"Thanks, Leo," said Ava. "But I had it under control."

"You call that under control?" asked Leo. He grinned and held Ava close. "Come on, let's go back to the sleigh."

Ava pushed Leo away and said, "No, I told you I have a plan. Just let me do this one thing." Leo just watched as Ava steadied her feet and leaped to Cupid.

"One more to go," Ava said to herself. The Sorrow King was now just a blur in the darkness ahead. Ava knew she couldn't make any more mistakes if she wanted her plan to work. She focused on Rudolph's glowing red nose. Her lungs filled with cold air as she tried to calm her nerves.

Ava made the last jump, this time landing right on Rudolph's back. She balanced herself and released the reindeer from the sleigh. Rudolph picked up speed and shot forward from the rest of the reindeer with Ava on his back. Ava fired a ball of ice as the pair approached the Sorrow King.

"You don't want this fight, little girl!" the Sorrow King shouted.

"Oh yes I do!" Ava pointed Lumina at the Despair Minions and fired another blast of ice. This time she didn't miss.

The twisted reindeer-shaped minion in front vaporized as the ice struck its midsection. The force of the blast caused the other minions to lose focus. Santa's sleigh lurched to the left, sending the Sorrow King crashing to the side. He yanked on the reins and steadied his Despair Minions.

"I warned you," said the Sorrow King. "But you would not listen. Time to say goodbye."

He released the reins just long enough to summon an orb of his dark magic and tossed it spinning towards Rudolph. Ava held on tight as the reindeer leaped over the orb. She used Lumina again to vaporize a second Despair

Minion. Then a third. The sleigh carrying the Sorrow King slowed to a crawl, allowing Santa, Leo, and the rest of the reindeer to catch up to the mid-air battle.

Leo had climbed back into the makeshift sleigh during Ava's attack. Now he stood on the edge, facing the Sorrow King, ready for a fight. Leo jumped off the side and landed on the Sorrow King's back. He swung Everblade hard and fast, striking the villain in the shoulder. The Sorrow King screamed in pain and lurched backward, throwing Leo to the floor of the sleigh.

"I thought I was tired of your silly games, elf," said the Sorrow King. "But now I am certain. Tell me, can you fly as well as Santa's reindeer?"

Leo struggled as the Sorrow King lifted him into the air and held him over the side of the sleigh. Leo swung Everblade in all directions, trying to land another blow. Rudolph swooped in from the side while Ava fired shot after shot. The Despair Minions became erratic, flying in all directions as they dodged the ice balls flying at them.

In the middle of the chaotic clash, the makeshift sleigh carrying Santa Claus collided with the Sorrow King, causing a violent crash. Metal and wood scattered through the air as the trio was thrown from the wreckage. Ava and Rudolph barely dodged the flying debris, only to watch their friends plummet through the night sky. Santa and Leo landed together on the frozen crust of the Dark Realm, while Santa's reindeer found their footing nearby. Back in control, the Sorrow King created a gentle wind that carried him to the ground just beyond Leo and Santa. Hundreds of Despair Minions appeared around him as he made contact.

"Do you surrender, Sorrow King?" asked Santa Claus.

"Surrender?" asked the Sorrow King. "I'm just getting started." He twisted his hands and pushed a cloud of dark magic forward. Santa called upon the ancient magic he had used so many times before, but no magic came to him. The cloud swallowed the jolly elf and trapped him inside.

"Your powers won't work here," said the Sorrow King. "Your precious Christmas Spirit is all gone, stashed away in the machine that your faithful elves joyfully built just for me."

"You don't have all of it!" a voice shouted behind the Sorrow King. Ava held the glowing scepter as she sat proudly atop Rudolph. "I have just one question for you, Sorrow King: Do you believe in the magic of Christmas?"

The Sorrow King sneered, "I believe in nothing but despair and darkness."

"Well, you will," said Ava.

She took a deep breath and summoned the remaining Christmas Spirit within her. Radiant light enveloped Ava and Rudolph as they glowed with the essence of pure joy and hope. She directed the light toward the crystal on Lumina and unleashed a flash, striking the hunk of metal that held the world's Christmas Spirit.

The machine turned white and began to shake and rattle. Screws and metal flew from every direction until the machine buckled under pressure. Instantly, the cold, dark night became bright and warm as the trapped Christmas Spirit poured out of the broken machine. The Sorrow King stared in horror as the world around him filled with joy and goodwill. The dark cloud that trapped Santa turned to dust and blew away. Santa and Leo were both enveloped by the Christmas Spirit and magic coursed through their bodies. The reindeer stomped their feet and whinnied with glee.

"Your dark reign ends now, Sorrow King!" said Santa Claus.

"Are you ready, Santa?" asked Leo.

"Let's show him the true meaning of Christmas," said Santa.

"Season's greetings, Sorrow King!" shouted Leo.

"Ho ho ho, Merry Christmas!" bellowed Santa Claus.

"What are you doing?" asked the Sorrow King.

"Oh, we're just spreading a little Christmas cheer," said Leo. "Tis the season to be jolly!"

"Have yourself a merry little Christmas!"

"Santa Claus is coming to town!"

"Stop it this instant!" cried the Sorrow King. He felt his grip on the Dark Realm weaken with every joyful phrase uttered by Leo and Santa. One by one, the Despair Minions vanished.

Leo and Santa approached the Sorrow King and continued their attack.

"We wish you a Merry Christmas!"

"May your days be merry and bright!"

"It's the most wonderful time of the year!"

Santa and Leo stood tall as the Sorrow King sank to his knees. Leo looked at his old friend and gave a friendly nod.

The guardian elf faced the weary Sorrow King, reached into the pocket of his tunic, and pulled out a pair of Giggle Goggles.

"What's the matter, Sorrow King?" asked Leo. "Are you not a fan of Christmas? Well, I have just the thing to change that."

"No, please! I beg you, not those miserable things again!"

Leo took the goggles and placed them on the Sorrow King's face. Laughter erupted from the evil brute as Leo pressed the goggles' button.

"Take them off!" the Sorrow King shouted between fits

of laughter. "I hate them!"

Santa took a deep breath and, with a twinkle in his eye, let out a resounding "Ho, ho, ho!" The joy in his voice echoed throughout the Dark Realm as it cut through the remaining Despair Minions. He knew the Sorrow King was nearly finished.

"Merry Christmas to all, and to all a good night!" cheered Santa.

The Sorrow King continued to laugh as his form slowly disappeared. Santa, Leo, and Ava all gathered around the defeated being. He looked up at them and smirked.

"I–ha ha ha–will rise–ha ha–again," he struggled to speak. "Even if–ha ha ha–it takes me–ha ha ha–a thousand years."

"We'll be waiting," said Leo. The Sorrow King laughed one last time before disappearing, overcome by the magic of Christmas.

The stolen Christmas Spirit had now filled the hearts of all who once believed in the magic of the season, restoring balance in all the realms.

"I believe this belongs to you," Ava said and handed Lumina back to Leo.

"You'll have to teach me your secrets when we get back home," said Leo. "Speaking of which…"

Leo reached into his tunic and pulled out the stone from

110

the Cave of Wonder.

"What do you have there, Leo?" asked Santa. "Another pair of Giggle Goggles?"

"This is our way out of this place," Leo said as he held up the stone. "Come on, let's go home."

Santa clicked his tongue. Rudolph, Vixen, Dasher, and the other reindeer came running. Ava and Santa placed their hands, along with Leo's, on the stone. Light poured from the stone and spread around them like a shimmering cocoon, as their surroundings began to shift and blur. They felt like they were floating through time and space.

As suddenly as it had begun, the glow faded, and they now stood on the snow-covered ground outside Santa's castle.

CHRISTMAS DAY

T he sun peeked over the hills, casting a soft golden light over the North Pole. Sparkles of light bounced off the ice-covered landscape. The crisp, cold air added to the peaceful scene.

Santa let out a hearty laugh. "We made it back!" he exclaimed, patting Rudolph and the other reindeer on their furry heads. The reindeer nuzzled Santa, expressing their relief at being back in familiar territory.

"We did it!" Leo said and looked around with a sense of wonder. "We're home!"

Ava beamed with pride, amazed that they had rescued Santa Claus and saved Christmas from the clutches of the Sorrow King.

Santa put his arm around Leo's shoulder.

"You two have done an incredible thing, my young friends," he said. "Your bravery has restored the true magic of Christmas and saved the world!"

"We couldn't have done it without each other," said Ava, smiling as she looked at Santa and Leo. "We make a great team!"

Santa Claus couldn't help but notice the state of his castle. The once majestic doors were now splinters and debris scattered about.

"My doors!" cried Santa. "Where have they gone?"

Leo and Ava locked eyes for a moment before Leo said, "Sorry, Santa. The Sorrow King trapped us inside and I had to destroy the doors to escape the castle."

"Don't worry, my boy." Santa placed a hand on Leo's shoulder. A smile played on his lips. "Sometimes sacrifices have to be made for the greater good, and you did what you had to do."

Mrs. Claus appeared in the archway where the doors once stood. A grin spread across her face as she noticed Ava, Leo, and Santa in the snow.

"Mr. Claus, you're back!" she exclaimed, rushing to greet her husband.

"Safe and sound, my dear," said Santa. "All thanks to these brave young heroes." Santa smiled and motioned to Ava and Leo.

113

Ava greeted Mrs. Claus with a warm smile. "It's good to see you, Mrs. Claus. We've brought Santa back—the real Santa—and the Christmas Spirit is back where it belongs."

Mrs. Claus hugged Ava and Leo. "Thank you both for saving Christmas and bringing back my dear Mr. Claus. The elves and I were worried sick," she said.

"Speaking of the elves, where have they gone?" asked Santa as he looked for the elves.

Ava took a deep breath and explained, "They were hiding under the floor in your study, Santa. The Sorrow King put them there, but Leo and I found them. Leo tried to get them to come out, but they refused."

"Under the floor?" said Santa. His eyes widened with concern. "We must free them immediately!" Santa rushed into the castle and led the way back to his study.

With Ava and Leo's help, Santa opened the trap door under the rug. The elves emerged, blinking in the light. Cheers and laughter filled the room as the elves celebrated, grateful to be free and back with their friends and family.

"My dear elves, I cannot tell you how proud I am of you," Santa said as he addressed the joyful crowd. "Although you all aided in the plot to destroy Christmas..." The crowd of elves frowned. "...You still performed your duties by following commands..." The elves smiled again. "...Even if those were the Sorrow King's commands."

"What can we do to make up for it?" asked an elf.

"My sleigh was destroyed in our battle with the Sorrow King. We must build a new one. A bigger one that can carry twice as many toys as the old one! Christmas cannot wait. Children all over the world are eagerly awaiting their gifts."

The elves nodded and set to work. They used their creativity to create a magnificent new sleigh, even more magical than the last. Ava and Leo chimed in with their ideas: Heated seats. A radio. A warming basket to store gingerbread cookies. Even a hot cocoa maker!

Santa marveled at the work and even gave a few hearty "Ho, ho, ho's" as the elves worked. They finished the new sleigh in no time. The elves cheered at their beautiful new design.

"You all did a fabulous job," said Santa. "Now fetch the presents from around the castle and load the sleigh! We must hurry! The good boys and girls of the world are waiting."

The Elder Elves called the beings of the North Pole to gather in Santa's castle. Ava and Leo stood in the center of the magnificent throne room surrounded by the elves of the castle, Santa and Mrs. Claus, the creatures of the Mystic Forest, and the Elder Elves.

"Leo, my guardian," said Santa. "And young Ava. We are all very pleased with what you two have accomplished. Without you, Christmas would have been lost to the Sorrow King. Your acts of bravery will live on for years to come."

Leo's face turned bright red at Santa's praise. "Ah, thank you, Santa Claus," said Leo. "But I only did what had to be done. Besides, I'm your guardian elf for a reason."

"You are not just Santa Claus's guardian," said Elder Oakbranch. "From now on, you will be named Protector of the Realms."

Leo smiled and waved as Santa's elves gave a huge cheer and applause for his new title. As the crowd calmed down, Leo knelt forward with one hand on his knee and the other outstretched.

"Thank you, Elder Oakbranch," said Leo. "I will always fulfill my duties as Santa's guardian and Protector of the Realms."

"And Ava," said Elder Willowbloom. "Your bravery has not gone unnoticed. From now on, you will be named Joybringer."

Ava tried to copy Leo's posture as best she could.

116

"Thank you, Elder Willowbloom," said Ava. "I promise to always do my duty as Joybringer."

The elves burst into another round of applause.

Santa chuckled and looked at Ava. "Now, dear Ava. It's almost time for us to take you home. Your father has been worried sick with you gone all this time."

"I understand, Santa," said Ava. "I'm ready to go home, even though I wish I could stay longer. Besides, isn't Christmas best spent with the ones you love?"

"Ho, ho, ho!" said Santa. "It certainly is."

"Santa, Elder Elves?" asked Leo. "Can Ava and I have a few minutes alone before we leave?"

Santa and the Elder Elves nodded their heads.

"Of course," said Santa. "I still have a list that needs checking twice. Come along, my dear elves."

The Elder Elves followed Santa as he rose from his great throne. The room slowly emptied, and the sounds of joyful chatter faded, leaving them with a moment of silence to share.

Leo took Ava's hands in his and looked into her eyes with sincerity.

"Ava, this has been an incredible adventure," he said. "I'm going to miss you."

"Do you think we'll ever see each other again?" asked Ava. "I don't want this to be goodbye forever."

Leo closed his eyes and thought. Then he had an idea. He reached into his tunic and in his hand was the stone they had used to escape the Dark Realm.

"Here, take this," he said, handing the stone to Ava. "Your powers should be able to make this work. You can visit me anytime you'd like!"

Her eyes widened as she stared at the magical stone now in her hands.

"Are you sure about this, Leo? What if you need it in an emergency?"

"I'm sure," he said. "Besides, I can always go to the Elder Elves if I need to travel somewhere far away."

Santa and Mrs. Claus poked their heads through the door.

"Ava, Leo," said Santa. "It's time."

"Okay," they both replied.

"But before we go," said Ava. "Is there any way I could try one of Mrs. Claus's famous gingerbread cookies?"

About the Author

Bradley Doxon grew up in a big house with a family that loved Christmas. It is his mother's favorite holiday, as it is now his.

Bradley lives with his wife and three children, two cats, and one dog far away from the North Pole.

https://www.bradleydoxon.com

If you liked the book you just read, please consider leaving a review. Reviews give indie authors like Bradley more inspiration to keep writing.

Printed in Great Britain
by Amazon